PENETRATION TESTING

A.H. CUNNINGHAM

*This Novella was originally part of the Current Anthology,
edited by Katrina Jackson and Tasha L. Harrison.
All the proceeds for the Anthology were donated to
organizations on the ground in Jackson, Mississippi, at the
height of their water crisis...which is still ongoing more than a
year later.*

CONTENT NOTES

This book depicts a scene where a character endures overstimulation in a public setting due to excessive sound.

CHAPTER
ONE

EMILE

The sun's rays woke me before my alarm, the unseasonable morning warmth seeping into the room and creeping into my bed. Right before I could reach the home pod, my alarm went off, signaling the beginning of another day.

One stretch, one good pull to make all my muscles pop and wake up, and I'd be ready for the day.

The home pod switched from the melodious alarm to my morning flow playlist, providing me the music to ease into the day. My feet sank into the soft wool of my rug as I let the daylight wake me up atom by atom.

This type of gentle morning routine was only made possible by the beauty of remote work. There were reasons I'd gravitated toward my chosen profession, one of them being the ability to work from home. With the type of personality I had, it was a perk that was imperative for my well-being.

After soaking in the sun streaming from the large windows in my bedroom, I padded toward my bathroom to shower and get my day going. Steam swirled around the bathroom as the hot water hit my shoulders. Damn, it had been a tense week. The integration testing on my client software had found several inconsistencies that needed to be addressed. I'd worked on coding the automated tests to cover all necessary angles, and after a nearly flawless unit of testing, I'd run into a wall.

The client called me every day to check about the release of their software. The copious notes I'd taken would probably not be welcomed even if they technically had asked for them. But that's why they paid me—to ensure their software worked well.

The good news, and the source of all my good humor, was that the tension I felt would dissipate today after my weekly afternoon appointment.

My massage appointment had me cheesing, glad I'd figured out eight months ago that I needed to make some strides to control my stress. One of the first steps I'd taken was hiring a weekly massage therapist.

The cheesing wasn't because of the relaxation, even though it was a welcome development, but because I got to talk to her again.

The Spanish I knew remained limited to questions about the location of the library and the restroom and asking how much something cost. However, I remembered from our Spanish classes in high school how Mr. Fernandez used to describe storms. He'd been completely in awe of the atmospheric phenomenon, drawing attention to the encompassing beauty of lightning and thunder, how the nimbus clouds formed to saturate the earth with water and coolness.

That's how I viewed her.

My massage therapist, Keyiara, had been the first person I took a chance on when I searched for a professional that did house calls, and once I met her, I knew not to look further.

Keyiara was a bright light illuminating the end of my week with smiles, chatter, and good company. Sometimes she'd be the only person I spoke to besides my brother in those weeks when I got lost in testing and coding to the point the days ran together.

Today promised to be one of those days. After a hearty breakfast, I sequestered myself in my office on the second floor of my loft. The room boasted full windows facing Williamsburg and my little neck of the woods. I fired up my computer and started the work of the day. After four hours of screen time, it was time to take a break. I'd implemented the breaks after my brother had taken me to task for always prioritizing work.

Just at the thought of my brother, his face flashed on the middle screen of my workstation composed of four screens and three keyboards. I pressed the green button.

"Yo! Emile, what's up? What you up to this weekend? Want to have dinner tonight, start the weekend right?"

Daymond asked. At a quick glance, I could tell he was in his office.

"What's up, D, how are you?"

"Nah, big bro, you don't get to brush off my invite."

"I'm older by four years. I'm hardly your big bro," I contested.

"Nah, you old, aren't you turning thirty-five? Son, that's old," Daymond said.

"Chill... I'm not old, just *older*."

"You've done such a good job of taking my attention away from the actual reason for my call," Daymond reminded me, and I grimaced.

"Man...listen."

"Nah, bruh, you listen. You gotta go out, explore more. You're such a hermit. Let's hit up a restaurant. Who knows what opportunities would find you—"

"I know what you're gonna say." I frowned even though D couldn't see me.

"Yes, so why you even have me saying it again?"

"I'm not. You know it's not a topic of discussion." The tenor of my voice shifted, and D knew me well enough to realize I was reaching the end of my rope for this conversation.

"It should be, though. You need to get out more. This is not the solution..."

"Listen, I'll hit you up later, alright?"

D scoffed. "Right, later, as in three days from now?"

"Nah, I'm down for dinner, but just dinner. I'm not going anywhere else,"

"Fine..."

"Later, D."

I was going to regret agreeing to go out in about five hours and would brainstorm a thousand ideas on how to get out of the plans, but I'd still attend because Daymond was right—lately, I had been staying home more. The few friends I had stopped inviting me out, already knowing what my answer would be.

My command center awaited me with all its screens, but a low hum of vibration began coursing through me as the time approached for my massage appointment. I sat at my desk and pulled up the timeline for this project, real-izing I was ahead of my own aggressive agenda to complete this early for my client.

Fuck it.

I strolled to my sofa, fired up my TV projector, searching to chase away the pulsations of nerves that threatened to make my skin itch.

The Photograph was already queued up, and I searched for the scene I wanted. Yeah, here it was—when Michael and Mae first have sex. It was one of my favorite movies, and the way their love story unfolded... A warm sensation found a path straight to my lower region as I rewound and watched the scene yet again.

If any of my guy friends—if *Daymond* ever were to find out I beat off to romantic movies...it would be a wrap for me. What kind of grown-ass man needs a romance flick to get off? Me. That's who.

After the first rewind, my movements increased, the

tension that had consumed me at the thought of my upcoming massage releasing as warm wetness hit my hand as I orgasmed.

That was better.

A quick shower, and I'd be ready for her arrival.

Now, I was prepared.

CHAPTER
TWO

EMILE

Her arrival at my apartment was always an event. Having had massages before her, I knew the therapist usually attempted to create a calming, quiet environment before, during, and at the end of the appointment.

Not Keyiara.

"My client favorito in Brooklyn!" A whirl of big curls and lushness waltzed into my home, the scent of verbena following with lemon trailing behind.

"Hey, Keyiara, how are you?'

"Ay, corazón, I've told you to call me Kiki like everyone calls me. How are you?" she said, immediately waking up all my senses. I moved toward her, ready to divest her of her travel massage bed, which she insisted on traveling with even though I'd offered a thousand times to buy my own one so she wouldn't have to slog it from Inwood to Williamsburg.

"No, no, see, my table is magic. It wouldn't be the same if you buy a new one," she'd always respond, brushing me off.

"I like your name, though." I shrugged and moved to set up the table by the window where the setting sun struggled to warm the cooling early evening.

Keyiara sauntered toward my kitchen, washing her hands in the sink with her soap and then whirling around so fast her hair took a second to catch up with her movement, whipping across her face.

"So, I think I'm getting closer!" She clapped her hands.

I hid a smile as I finished setting up the table, then turned to her.

"For real?" I lifted an eyebrow, knowing what came next.

"Actually, not like finish line close, but definitely a half a mile closer." Her bottom lip caught between her perfect teeth as she shrugged.

"That's what's up! So, when do I get to try this aphrodisiac weed concoction of yours?"

"Ugh, I'm going to demote you as my favorite client in Brooklyn!" she said with a pout.

"I'm pretty certain you have complained enough to me about me being the only client you have in Brooklyn," I reminded her.

"Right. Well, I told you, they are cannabis love bites.

That's how you should call them—Kiki's Cannabis Love Bites." She flashed her hands as if drawing a marquee in the air. Keyiara had been working on these recipes since the first day I met her almost a year ago, and she still wasn't fully satisfied with her results.

"So, when am I gonna try these, though? Maybe I can help tell you what's missing." I turned around to remove my shirt, following the usual steps of this dance of ours we had perfected every Friday when Keyiara showed up for my four-thirty appointment.

"No, no, I can't have you taste it yet. They don't have all the magic built in yet."

"Magic," I admonished, shaking my head.

She pointed her finger at me, shaking it. "No, no, no, calla. You know I've told you they have magic, and magic is all about intent."

"I thought you said it wasn't magic."

"Well, yeah, I use the word magic for lack of a better term, but my Metresa, she's getting me closer and closer."

At this point, all her rapid-fire words made sense to me. It had taken me a couple of months to fully follow the long stream of consciousness that she'd impart without one ounce of shyness.

The first time she'd rattled off telling me about her Metresa, I'd been very confused. I hated confusion and lack of knowledge, so I'd investigated until I had a better understanding of her belief in the syncretic religion.

"That's what's up. So, when you get another mile, I'll get to try them. How's your family?" I rested against the windowsill, waiting for when she'd be ready to start. With Keyiara, four-thirty was just a suggestion to show up at my apartment. Depending on the week, she would tell me about her day or her week for over thirty minutes before we started the appointment.

It was a source of hilarity for Daymond that his strict, taciturn older brother had found himself the chattiest massage therapist to relieve his stress. Before meeting Keyiara, I'd agree, but now? Well, this was the highlight of my week.

At my question about her family, her sepia tone illuminated to a burnt golden glow.

"They're good, everyone is good. Well, Abu has another cold…" She frowned with her whole body, her eyebrows and shoulders lowering, her mouth flattening, her eyes crinkling in concern. Then before I could offer words of support, she morphed back to her happy place.

"But she's resilient; you know my Abu will outlive us all. Enough about me, how are you? How's the timeline for the new project?"

"Progressing at pace."

She grinned as she rested her lower body against the kitchen island.

"You always sound so serious and exact. No extraneous words for Mr. Walker."

"Emile."

"I gotta keep some level of professionalism, Emile." She kept grinning as she padded her way toward me. The yellow polish on her toes glinted in the light, making the encounter feel much more intimate than it really was. But then again, Keyiara was about to run her warm, soft palms all over my body...

"Nonsense. We lost all levels of professionalism when you told me you wanted to create food bites to get people horny and slightly high. If I well remember, that was the third appointment," I said with a straight face, and she paused to cackle, her curls bouncing as she took my words for exactly what they were, a harmless joke.

Few people understood my humor and dry wit. But she did. She got it from day one.

"You right, you right. Damn, son, you don't miss one, do you?"

"Nope, I don't." And with that, I made my way to the massage table.

The second my body hit the warmth of Keyiara's magical travel bed, I knew things would change.

"Are you ready?" Keyiara's voice lowered to that sultry tone she deemed relaxing but lately had become distracting. She gave a command, and my lights dimmed.

"What scent today?"

"Sandalwood."

"Yum, excellent choice. You got a date?" she asked as she lit a couple of candles unearthed from her bag of tricks.

"Why you ask that?" I wondered, startled by her question.

"Don't know... Usually, you ask for that scent when you have a date or a lady friend."

"I tell you too much."

"Oh, please, the little I know I have pried out of you at high cost." Her laugh tickled my ears, traveling inside me, igniting that same vibration I thought I'd worked out of my system.

"High cost?"

"Yeah, a lot of personal information and a lot of corny jokes. Ok, don't distract me anymore," she whispered, and the click of the massage oil cap signaled the actual start of the appointment.

ABOUT A YEAR AGO, I'd gone for my regular doctor's checkup, and he'd advised my blood pressure was slightly elevated. Frustration had threatened to take over at the news. I did all the right things. He knew my habits; I did taekwondo in the evenings, ran on the weekends, and ate a balanced diet, but the one thing I didn't have fully under control was my stress levels.

I tried yoga, but it was harder than I thought, and I struggled with the feeling of so many people close to me practicing at the same time. I tried meditation, but my mind would wander into coding. Then my brother Daymond recommended massage sessions. He knew Keyiara from his friend group and thought it would be a good fit.

And what a good fit.

My muscles were currently undergoing a transformation from solid to malleable under Keyiara's expert hands. After months of sessions, she applied the perfect pressure to my back and shoulders as she worked on my knots.

While she worked, she hummed. If she found a particularly hard knot, the hum would deepen in disapproval, a sign she felt I wasn't doing enough self-care during the week. Her higher, faster-paced buzzes announced when she hit a particular stride in a muscle or area she felt was behaving exactly as it should. And when her hands ventured closer to my ass clad in sweatpants, a cute little staccato purr would begin until she pressed my gluteus.

Today she lingered as her hand trailed toward my buttocks. As flashes of earlier assaulted me, the usual calm that fell on me at this stage failed me. By now, I'd have fallen into a sleepy trance, but not today. Today, I remained aware of the verbena and her deep breathing and her hums of pleasure as she kneaded my ass, then ran her hands down my sweatpants.

"I haven't done your legs in detail in a while," she said in a low voice.

I bet.

In the beginning, I'd done these naked with a sheet covering me. I had zero concerns regarding untimely erections as I didn't work that way. The code that opened my arousal wasn't a simple touch, and strangers couldn't elicit that type of lust in me, so I hadn't bothered with any concerns.

But lately…

"Yeah, we can try next week," I murmured as she continued down my legs to massage my calves.

"Ok, but it's not the same with clothes on... But you have to be comfortable. I won't pressure you," she replied, continuing her ministrations.

Her warm breath caressed my foot as she worked on the sole, and I shifted on the table. Things were getting uncomfortable. This hadn't happened before, not to this extent. A chubby was the most I'd had to endure, but I was well on my way to a full erection.

Fuck.

The coding for the integration test... Yeah, I would focus on that. I ran the steps through my mind as Keyiara's hands danced over my body back toward my shoulders.

"You're so tense; what were you doing this week?" she asked, not expecting an answer, and the heat of her body kissed my back, the lingering weight of her heavy breasts teasing my muscles. What would it feel like to have her press completely against me?

Warm puffs of her breath tickled the back of my neck as she worked on the stubborn knots of my stressful week. Integration week always took the best out of me.

Her breath was audible, and I imagined what it would be like to surge inside of her as she hummed and panted in my ear... No, that way lay madness.

Back to work thoughts. The two error reports I needed to work on had to be finished first thing Monday to move forward with—

Her hands ghosted over my flanks, and the touch made me shiver.

"Are you cold?"

"Nah, I'm straight," I replied, hoping my body wouldn't betray me any further.

"Ok, it's time to turn."

She tapped my right shoulder. But I couldn't do it. I didn't know if I could keep things under control. I'd thought enough about work to get me back to a semi, but I was teetering on the edge of inappropriate.

"Come on, sleeping beauty," she said, nudging my shoulder, making me follow her instructions, helpless but to obey. And she thought I was sleeping.

She couldn't be more wrong.

The cap clicked open again, and the sound of the oil squelching as she rubbed her hands stimulated me further. She stood by the top of the table, and as every Friday, she ran her palms from my shoulders down to my pectorals and back up, massaging the muscles. But unlike most Fridays, goosebumps erupted in her path.

Her soft belly cradled the top of my head, and I would have loved to snuggle all the way into her generous curves. My mind ran away from me, no discipline behind any of my thoughts as she glided her hands in practiced moves on my needy flesh. Images of a naked, lush Keyiara massaging my body, both of us oiled up, took over, a full-length movie of heat, wetness, and passion. Then the worst happened—my body joined the mutiny.

"Oh, Dios mio, esta inmenso," Keyiara whispered as

my dick gave her a full salute inside my sweatpants. And why did I translate that sentence with such ease? I didn't remember Mr. Fernandez teaching us that. Desperation crept over me as I turned fully tumescent, my heavy flesh lengthening down my leg, searching for release.

"Fuck, I'm sorry! This is…"

She hadn't stopped touching me. Throughout my dick going fully erect, she'd kept at it, but her touch had changed from the firm kneading to a luxurious caress, her fingers trailing over my nipples and then further down my abs, my spine tightening. She trailed dangerously close to…

Fuck no, no, no!

A ball of tension popped and unleashed inside me. Hot release escaped me, quickly turning lukewarm as a wet spot grew on my sweatpants.

"Oh my god, that was…" she said in wonderment.

"Fucking embarrassing." "Hot as fuck." We mumbled in unison.

I jerkily sat up, pushing her hands away as I attempted to cover the spot that kept growing as she stared at it. I splayed my hands like a starfish over my crotch. All the relaxation she'd elicited escaped me in less than a second. I was probably imagining the way her eyes clouded and her nose widened as she took shallow breaths, and what was her chest doing, rising and falling so…emphatically?

"Listen, you better go. I'm sorry for this. This was inappropriate of me," I said, shifting my gaze to her face, where her glazed stare had me second-guessing myself for a second. But no, it had to be the residual lust that was making me imagine things. Keyiara was...not for the likes of me.

"I...I'm so—"

"No, no, it's ok. Listen, I'll call you. Let's take a break next week."

"A break?" Finally, her trance broke, and she stared at me clearly.

I nodded, grabbing my t-shirt where I'd folded it on the sofa and propelling my way toward the door.

She trailed me with her gaze, then shrugged as if unbothered by the entire situation.

In seconds, she packed up, her travel table back in its backpack contraption.

"You sure you don't want me to stay?" she asked bluntly.

"No, I've already put you in an untenable position." I knew she was just trying to be nice.

She sighed.

"Men," she mumbled and breezed past me, leaving me to stew in my embarrassment.

CHAPTER

THREE

KEYIARA

The A train chugged along, and I was lucky to be sitting down in the middle of rush hour on a Friday afternoon. Shock and awe still coursed through my veins as I tried to wrap my mind around what had just gone down in my favorite client's condo.

The need to debrief threatened to keep me in a chokehold the entire ride home. Pulling out my cell phone, I fired off a quick text.

Me: Girl I need to talk!

Juju: If you are on the train, don't you dare call me.

Ugh, this girl. We could not be more different. I mean, on the surface, we were similar—both opinionated plus-size Black women with Caribbean heritage, her Jamaican, mine Dominican Republic. But that's where the similarities ended.

I loved where I was in life even though I was always working on something new; she was eternally threatening to leave New York City but didn't do one thing differently in her day-to-day. But we were each other's sounding board—we've known each other since we were toddlers, and our moms worked in the same daycare. She always worried so much about what people thought, and she refused to get on the phone with me if I was riding the train. It tempted me to dial her just to fuck with her, but I needed her full attention right now.

Me: Fine. Big dark Lindt got a rise out of his massage today.

I tapped my feet to the rhythm of the bachata flowing through my earbuds. The Friday night energy vibrated through the train passengers. Even in a city like this where there was no downtime, Friday night still held vast possibilities, and the body just tapped into that vibe.

Juju: Wait what? Mr. Brooklyn? What did you do to that sweet soul?

Me: Girl bye. I didn't do anything different from every other Friday.

But, I'd had different thoughts and energy today than the other days. I might have followed each of the steps of my regular choreography with Emile, but I certainly had seasoned my intentions differently.

The train slowed down toward the next stop, and the jostle of bodies had me clutching my belongings lest someone tried something slick and met the wrong one.

Juju: So, what did you do?

Me: Nothing. Well, I wanted to offer some help because... Juju he's built, built like the man of my dreams.

Juju: I'mma ignore the objectifying. You said he's not your type.

That's right, he wasn't. Because he was quiet and taciturn, and I'd probably have him eating out of the palm of my hand, and... I needed to be challenged. I like me the bad boys; I didn't want to play games, but somehow game players found me. And I loved it.

Me: yeah, girl but I wouldn't mind taking a spin, you know?

JuJu: Girl, don't go planning on breaking that man's heart.

The train was fast approaching Dykeman, and I was fast approaching my limit for this conversation. Somehow Juju had turned this into something more serious, and I wished I'd kept my news to myself.

I answered back a simple acknowledgment, then departed the train at my stop. La Dykeman pulsated with the same Friday energy that coursed through my veins, that intent to live life to the fullest if only for a few hours until the sun rose again.

Instead of going home, I made my way to the apartment across the street from mine, knowing I'd find my partner in crime there.

"Abu, tu 'ta en casa?" I shouted as I opened the door to my Mai and Abu's apartment to immediately be assaulted by the potent smell of tobacco.

"Niña, why you scream so loud? I'm right here!" Abu

sat in her rocking chair right in the living area, next to the altar of our Metresa Anaisa de Pye. She had a beer in her hand and was smoking, a hypnotic sway to her brown hand as it hovered between her drink and her cigar.

"Abu, no smoking in the house. What are you asking Anaisa that you are smoking and drinking beer?"

"I'm asking for you to get what you need instead of what you want," Abu said in her cryptic manner. Right. This was something she did some days to my mom or me —she'd have what I could only describe as visions, but if you asked her were intense moments where she connected with us and got a glimpse of what we needed.

"Alright, Abu, but make sure you ask her to help me get the perfect recipe for my love bites."

"I don't ask for what I already know will be." She scoffed and put out her cigar, stomping her legs on the floor and standing up in one swoop, beer in hand. The strength of her always left me in awe.

"Abu..." I started as my mom marched into the living room, her face scrunched up in disapproval.

"Aqui viene la gruñona," Abu whispered. Mai marched over to us. I took after my father's side of the family with a plus-size body that ignored all the miles I walked a day but couldn't pass up storing the extra mangu I ate on weekends. Abu was also a large woman, with the type of arms and elbows that told you that you'd think of her cooking for months to come. Mai, on the other hand, resembled a broad-billed tody, but a mean one when mad, and she always tried to keep Abu and me in line to dubious success.

"Mama! Por favor, I've asked you not to smoke that nasty stuff in the house. If you must smoke it, go to Kiki, she has that blasphemous altar in her apartment as well." Mai glared at Anaisa while Abu and I exchanged a quick glance.

"Mai, don't be mad at her, and you know that Anaisa is just Santa Ana."

"Sí, and I'm the queen of England," Mom clapped back. I wasn't invested in arguing with her when I just wanted to gossip with Abu. "Y tú qué? Shouldn't you be heading home so you can open the restaurant mañana? You must be there by five, you promised you could open."

"Sí, Mai, I promised you I'd open so you can get some rest. Ya, bájale." I stopped her fussing with a big hug, giving her a kiss on the top of her head. She softened her stance, letting me give her some love and receive in return.

Once I let her go, I made a quick eyes-only communication with Abu and got her to follow me to the kitchen while Mai stayed behind, airing the living room and beating all the sofa cushions to oblivion as if that would chase away the smell of the cigar.

"Que lo que, niña?" Abu asked me the moment we stepped into the kitchen.

"Abu, 'ta grande. You won the bet," I said, trying to gauge between my hands the size of Emile's...gift.

"Oh jo! I knew it! I want my fifty bucks. But how?" Abu asked in a shorthand that worked well for both of us.

"Abu, he got hard while I was massaging him. I was this close to asking him if he wanted help with that. I tell you, I'm still in awe."

"I told you, you need a man like that, not like those little friends you like messing with who like to play games and keep you waiting at night by the phone. That's not a man, niña, that's a boy. But that client of yours? That's un tigerazo."

"Ay, Abu, you know I can't date men like him. He's so nice, and I love his sense of humor, but he's taciturn and... he's just not my type."

"Bah, type, que type? You've told me he's big all around, and you know, with big-boned women like us, that matters. But all of that is superficial. The important thing is he listens to you, and you love talking to him. Almost a year, and every Friday after your appointment, you walk through the front door glowing." Abu raised her perfectly arched eyebrow, then wiggled it for better effect. The sudden tightening of my belly at her words shed light on feelings I'd done my best to ignore for the past months.

"Ugh, but besides, he got super awkward after it all and told me he wanted to take a break, so who knows? This might be the last time I see him."

"Mhm...we'll see." Abu pursed her mouth, then took a swig of her beer, finishing the drink.

FOUR

EMILE

The crisp fall air made me wish I'd worn a thicker sweater. I'd assumed the sun would keep me warm enough as I sat on the sidelines, watching Daymond and some of our friends warm up before their baseball game started.

Daymond had been nudging me for a few weeks to come and see him play in this new league in Inwood Park he'd joined, but I hadn't had the time nor the inclination. Now that I'd finished my latest assignment, I figured he wouldn't take any more excuses. And I needed to get out of my space. It had been four weeks—not that anyone was counting, especially not me—that I hadn't seen her. To be fair, the reason sat squarely on me; after spontaneously ejaculating like a fifteen-year-old, I couldn't imagine facing her again.

Keyiara reached out after the first week, asking if we were back on track with our sessions. I responded by explaining the deadline of my current assignment had been moved up, which was true, and that I couldn't afford to waste any time, which was partially true, so I'd call her when I was ready to resume our sessions. That had been a bald-faced lie.

She sent me one more text message the Friday after that exchange asking if I was at least meditating and taking time for myself. I responded with a thumbs up.

This was why I failed at any type of interpersonal relationship outside of the ones I'd established during school. Those few close friends I had didn't have a choice but to spend time with me because of proximity. In that proximity, they'd gotten to know the whole me, not just the first outer impression that was hard to crack.

"Yo! E, daydreaming again? Listen, JJ won't make it on time for the game. Can you play for him till he arrives?" Daymond trotted my way with a glove extended to me.

"Catcher? I can do that." I shrugged and accepted the glove from him, following behind.

I KNELT behind home plate as the game started, Daymond pitching the bottom of the first inning. The league had a five-inning game structure which I was glad for because if JJ flaked, I still didn't have to invest my whole day out here in the park. I signaled D to throw a curveball, to which he complied, the beauty of his technique showing as the ball flew right into my glove. *Out.* The synergy between D and I was unmatched. This was the one game our dad had taught us since we were in diapers, the only time he took a moment to bond with the two with us.

Hard work was the currency Jacob Walker believed opened doors, and he'd taken that mentality in every aspect of his life. He'd also made sure Daymond and I understood that at home, a man's job was to work hard, be silent, and be supportive. The right woman would see these good qualities and fall in love. Daymond had been the smarter one of the two of us, taking Dad's advice as a suggestion with its flaws and all versus how I'd internalized the message.

Five to five at the bottom of the fifth inning, and JJ was nowhere to be found. I strolled onto base with my bat. "Vamos, Emile!!" boomed from the few bleachers around the field, the cheer jostling my heart. Not wanting to break my concentration, I didn't look around for the source, but that voice... I knew that voice.

The pitcher tried a fastball, a thrill rushing through me at the ping of the ball connecting with the metal bat, signaling a hit. The ball flew through the air, and I took off, feet pounding the ground, air whistling in my ears, as I sprinted to first, then second base. The ball fell somewhere between second and third, but their outfielder was eating shit and missed the catch.

"Yes! That's how we do it! Come on, Emile!" Again, that voice. I bumped fists with the dude in second, then got into my ready stance, waiting for the next batter, who just so happened to be D. I knew D was gonna hit it out of the park, so I needed to be ready. But my gaze betrayed me, and I quickly searched the bleachers to find Keyiara's big smile, her head full of curls. My heart underwent a series of repeated jumps, the speed of my beats faster than my run to base.

She wore a long-sleeved gray sweater dress that show-cased her thick thighs and wrapped over her lush body the same way I'd dreamed I could wrap around her. These lustful thoughts and dreams were not the norm for me, and the way she had me masturbating...yeah, all the way out of the norm. I hadn't felt this way since my girlfriend in freshman year of college.

Laughter and nudges ensued when Keyiara's friends realized the direction of my gaze, and she immediately shut things down by waving and winking at me. Right after that, they went back to focusing on the game, which I'd stopped doing just in time to miss D's hit.

I pushed, using my momentum all the way to home plate to the cheers of the bleachers, dapping Daymond up when he reached home plate as well. We'd won the game.

I ventured a glance at where Keyiara and her friends were sitting, and they were standing up, cheering the loudest. I ignored the way my chest tightened at the sight of Keyiara's laughter and how it felt better than winning.

"Oh, that's Kiki, JJ's cousin. How did she show up, but he flaked? And why's Kiki so invested in yo' game?"

Daymond asked as we walked to the bullpen to get our cellphones and keys.

"You forget you introduced me to Keyiara."

"I did? Oh, right, your massage therapist! You always call her 'my massage therapist,' so it slipped my mind." I grabbed my stuff as D chatted it up with minimal input from me.

As we strolled out of the pen, Keyiara and her friends approached us, my skin tightening as they came near. Damn, I really should have layered today.

"Hi, Emile," she greeted me, her face completely animated, and as always, some of my reticence flew away in her presence.

"Hey, Keyiara. This is my brother, Daymond. I believe you know each other."

"What's doin', Daymond? These are my girls, Juju and Lira."

Juju waved with a straight face, and Lira smiled and nodded. I returned the greeting.

"So, it takes me coming to see my cousin play to run into you? I didn't know you hung out in Inwood." She expertly maneuvered me away from the rest of the group as my brother made the ladies laugh with his antics.

"I don't. D convinced me to come today." I shrugged, deeply cognizant of how close she stood. I'd been closer to her in many ways this past year, but this new awareness, this yearning...it was disconcerting.

"Oh, I see. So, this is a one-time thing?" she asked curiously.

"Why, do you come out here often?"

"*Me?* This is my park. I live in walking distance to here."

"That's what's up. I don't think I knew you stayed here. I assumed…"

"Washington Heights, probably, which is close enough." It was her turn to shrug, her entire being moving to express herself. She'd probably be able to have an entire conversation through body language.

"But there you go, answering questions with questions." She waved at me, shaking her head.

"I didn't mean to. What I was gonna say is yes, I plan to come again. D is close to convincing me to join the league," I said, surprising myself. Daymond had started a campaign for me to join, but it wasn't until this moment that the idea had merit.

"Well, we're the official cheerleaders of the league, and especially the Warriors as JJ and Juju's brother Ephraim play on that team."

"Well, I'll be a Warrior too," I said and pumped my chest out for her, then wondered what had gotten into me.

"So, my task here is done. I've convinced you to do another activity that doesn't involve you sitting in front of a computer," she said, placing her hand over one of my trapeziuses. It was as if her hand had pressed all over my body, the way every single molecule froze in attention.

"Tsk, tsk… Four weeks without me, and you are a knotty mess."

If only she knew.

"Yeah, sorry, I just needed to finish this project."

"So, you finished it now?" She tilted her head, her eyes flashing with something I didn't want to explore too closely. I knew this woman was way out of my reach.

"I...did." I didn't have it in me to lie.

"So?" She crossed her arms over her chest, her sweater dress shifting slightly, exposing more of her silky brown skin. Why were these details suddenly registering with me?

"Yeah, come by next Friday..." I said in a monotone that I hope didn't betray my absolute excitement to see her again.

Keyiara narrowed her eyes at me, then pursed her glossy lips.

"Listen, I'm not trying to pressure you to do anything you're not comfortable with. If you prefer, I can give you a recommendation for another therapist."

"No!" My heart seized at the mere thought of someone else in my space, someone that wasn't Keyiara.

"You don't look too enthused about my services." She doubled down her stance, raising an eyebrow and tilting her head to the side.

She didn't need to know how enthused she made me.

"Nah, you know me, I'm just a bit..." I shrugged again, not sure what to do with my arms as if they had suddenly grown larger than I could handle.

Her gaze softened, and she uncrossed her arms. The way her body told me she understood didn't require additional words.

"I figure bringing up what happened would be best, so I just want to assure you that it's a normal reaction, and I'm a professional."

Great, I was just like her other clients; that's just what a dude wants to hear. Also, nothing that had happened after I got hard was professional—not that I'd ever call her out on it; I started it.

"Ok, come through, same time."

"See you next week, my favorite client in Brooklyn!"

FIVE

KEYIARA

The heat of the kitchen radiated on my skin, anticipation making me stare at my watch for each second getting me closer to the time I could open the oven door.

"Why are you standing here in the heat like this was a sauna?" Abu asked, strolling into the kitchen.

"Abu, don't start with me. Nothing is going to mess with my day today." I'd woken up with a tingling in my fingers and a sense of endless possibility in the back of my brain. There had been a few days in my life that I'd woken up feeling the same—one was when I came up with the idea for Kiki's Cannabis Love Bites, another was the day I found out the apartment I rented was going on sale and I could afford it. One of them was when Abu had taken me under her wing to teach me all her knowledge, and there was when Mai and Dad hooked up after being divorced for a few years. They were still separated, but they had moved from divorced to complicated.

"I know," Abu agreed with my positive intention.

My phone went off right in that instant, and my heart skipped a beat. I don't know what I was looking for the cannabis bites to taste like. All the previous attempts had been delicious, and everyone had enjoyed them, but I still felt something was missing. I wasn't certain what it was, but sometimes it wasn't about the ingredients; it was about the intent and the mind frame while mixing all the ingredients together.

The blaze of the oven grazed my face as I grasped the tray with the bites. The scents of chocolate and maca swirled in the kitchen with an undertone of sweet herb.

"This is close. You should take it to your client to taste."

"What? No, not yet. I must make sure it's the *final* final, you know?"

I cut a piece of the baked concoction and bit into the fluffy cake, the taste of chocolate dissolving in my mouth. I'd finally managed the right ratio of sweet and salty, the aftertaste an invitation to try more.

"See, you know this is close. Take to him," Abu insisted, and I shook my head.

"Nah, Abu, you're over here plotting on me, but I promise, this story doesn't have the end you think."

"You know I wasn't born ayer, right?" She closed a fist on her ample hip, stealing a bite and popping it into her mouth. Her eyes brightened, and a smile emerged once she finished chewing.

"I'm going to take a few of these to Mr. Devonte," she said, referring to the owner of the Jamaican bakery next to our restaurant.

"Abu!!" I exclaimed, scandalized. No matter how much Abu and I gossiped and cackled together, it was still hard to wrap my mind around the fact she still had a fulfilling sexual life. I mean, good for her, but still, this was my grandma.

"What? When you are my age, you'll remember this conversation. Now, don't forget, before you go to your client today, take him a bite."

I STOOD outside of Emile's apartment, wondering if I should have listened to Abu. But no, I was supposed to be here and be professional. Things had already gone off the rails with me and Emile in our last session, and bringing him one of the cannabis bites would probably be the incorrect message to send. I rarely cared about words like professionalism because it was usually masked in the package of doing things a certain way that didn't speak to who I was, but I knew Emile thought differently.

I knocked on his door and waited. No response. Usually, he was quick to open. Odd. I knocked again.

There was a noise coming from inside that sounded

like a wounded animal. Did Emile get a puppy or something?

Weird.

"Emile, are you there?" I raised my voice and knocked again.

I heard footsteps now. He opened the door and...

"Are you ok?" I blurted out. Emile's brow was scrunched up, and his lips were tightly closed.

"Come in," he grunted, barely opening his mouth.

"Umm...are you sure?"

He shrugged and waddled away from the door. I was tempted to leave, but he looked to be in pain, walking like he had a sack of rocks between his legs.

"Are you alright?" Something wasn't right. Emile had stopped by the large sofa in his living room, his back to me, a slight stoop to his usually erect stance.

"I'm fi— Fuck. I meant to call you to cancel."

This...

"Listen, Emile, you and I have always gotten along. I get that you were embarrassed about what happened last time, but I'm gonna need you not to play with my time or my money."

"I was gonna cancel because I'm in pain," he gritted out as he clutched the back of the sofa.

"Oh, what's hurting you? Maybe I can massage it and make it better?" I asked, feeling a little guilty I'd gone off on him until he barked a laugh that sounded like that noise I'd heard earlier.

So, he was the wounded animal.

"Trust me, you can't massage this away," he muttered, walking around the sofa to gingerly sit on the chair. The way he moved reminded me of the time I had lightning crotch pain and had to go to the doctor to figure out what was happening.

I approached the sofa, wondering why he wasn't going to urgent care or something. I'd be in a rideshare by now.

"Can I sit?"

"Yeah, yeah," he said, but I could swear it sounded like, "No, no."

I hesitated, wondering if I should just leave, but he looked in pain, and I couldn't leave him like this.

"Come on, let me take you to urgent care," I said instead of sitting down.

"No, I know what it is. I know what they'll say." He groaned, his fist holding onto the cushions.

"What is it?" The intrigue threatened to kill me as he sat there, face completely contorted in pain, not saying a word.

Emile gnawed his bottom lip, avoiding my gaze as I waited. I sat down on the armchair across from him, wanting to give him some space.

"Epididymal hypertension."

"Epi-what?" *The fuck was that?*

"Blue balls." He grumbled in annoyance.

"Oh. *Oh*... Oh!"

His gaze finally found mine, and the pain and challenge in them made me want to jump in, eyes closed, and worry about the repercussions after.

"There's only one solution to that."

"Yes, there is, but I'm so in pain, I couldn't do it."

"Well, I did say I could massage and make it better." I chuckled and licked my lips, my mouth suddenly parched.

"For real? Nah, I can't ask you to do that. I'm not that type of dude," he said, seeming as flustered as I felt.

"I... Well, this wouldn't be work." I shook my head. "I want to be clear, this is just me helping a friend."

"A friend, huh?" He grunted and shifted on the sofa, and how had I not paid attention to the fact that he was shirtless and wearing basketball shorts? I'd been so focused on his pain that I'd missed the expanse of beautiful dark skin.

"Yeah, I... I just want to..."

He pushed off the sofa in a fluid movement, and I tilted my head up to keep my eye on him. In a swift move, he dropped his basketball shorts.

Yeah, things were looking dire. A thrill of anticipation ran through me, the tingle in my fingers from the morning returning, urging me to act.

"Stand over here." I lowered my voice, afraid to spook him if I said anything else.

He never broke eye contact with me as he stood in front of me, his gaze full of embarrassment and excitement. I touched him, my grasp sure, and he startled.

"Sorry, I didn't want to scare you." He was so warm in my hand, and the girth...oh my.

"You didn't. I'm good."

"Are you, though?" I chuckled again as I ran my hand

up and down his length. "Do you have anything... like...aid?"

He stared at me, and I realized he was probably too gone, so I quickly unzipped my bag and pulled out the sandalwood oil.

"Oh."

"Yeah." I smiled and squirted some oil on my hands.

I stroked up and down his penis. It was a work of art with smooth skin his same dark complexion and a mushroom head slightly lighter in color. I imagined gliding my mouth up and down his dick, but I restrained myself from crossing that line. The only thing we had agreed to was me helping him with my hand, and that's what I would do.

His moans and groans marked the speed of my strokes. My instinct would have been to tease, to prolong the pleasure, but Emile needed quick release, and I was happy to provide that. He grew even more in the palm of my hand as I kept up my strokes. With my other hand, I caressed his balls, hoping my touch would give him some release. The lubrication kept the strokes smooth, and soon, Emile was thrusting into my fist.

"Fuck, this is so much better than my hands," he mumbled, and I grinned. All this stimulation and thrusting had my underwear transforming to liquid, my pussy throbbing in response to his alluring groans.

"I... I think I'm..." he choked out, and a stream of warm white liquid shot out of his dick, hitting my chest and my arm.

"Oh fuuuck," he moaned, his body quivering as he finally released himself.

He went utterly quiet once he reached his climax, and I craved to reach mine. I stood up, taking off my tank top and revealing my bra. I hadn't worn anything sexy today, but my brown demi cup would do.

"What...what are you... Damn, you are..." Emile started blabbering, his dick going soft between us. A girl could get used to the attention.

"I figured we'd finish what you started," I said, throwing all caution to the wind and reaching back to unclasp my bra.

"Wait!" He stopped me, holding my hands in front of me.

"What happened?" I stared at him and suddenly worried I had moved too fast. I was two seconds from going from aroused to pissed, so he better start explaining.

"I... Listen, I don't... I can't... I'm—" He broke eye contact with me, then searched around his loft as if the words he needed were floating around us.

"Fine, you don't want to fuck. That's alright." I yanked my arm from his grasp, my cheeks warming. I'd assumed he wanted more than just release. Silly me.

His soft touch underneath my chin compelled me to look at him. Getting lost in his deep brown eyes, my stomach shuffled a one-two bachata step, and I wondered why I hadn't had a glass of water in a minute.

"Nah, don't get it twisted, I'd love to fuck you. I just... I never done *it* before," he said, voice strong and sure, his last words resonating around and inside of me.

Something told me not to react in awe. I'd known Emile for a while now; he was proud, sensitive, and intensely private. What he'd just shared with me... I knew not to take the gesture lightly.

"Ok, I get it. Jumping into it right away would be disconcerting." I nodded, keeping my tone even.

He searched my face, then chuckled.

"Thanks for reacting this way, but you can express yourself now."

Oh, THANK GOD.

"You, Emile Walker, sexy computer whiz, have never had sex before? How on earth?" I exclaimed, letting all my excitement flow out of me.

"Yeah, that's more like it." He grinned, then messed with his diamond earring. Oh no, he was nervous. He hadn't done that around me in a while. During the first months of knowing each other, he would do it occasionally, but it hadn't happened in such a long time. I grabbed his right hand and pressed it to my chest, his warm palm nestling in my cleavage. *Oh, that felt too good.*

"I just want you to know that this, what you told me, stays with me. And...it hasn't changed how I feel about wanting to...you know..." I trailed off, wondering if his touch had transferred his nervousness to me. I wasn't usually this hesitant.

"I... Yeah, well, I've tried, and it's never worked. I

mean, I think I can do casual, but it has to still be meaningful, you feel me?

Did I feel him? He stood naked, a breath away from me, his heat teasing my skin, his scent seducing me to step closer, his eyes tempting me to get lost in the moment.

"I get it. It can't be transactional, got it." I nodded, not knowing what else to say.

"How about we take a few days to cool down? Figure out if this is where we really want to take things?"

"Alright," I agreed, but inside, there was a riot going on, especially in my lower region. This man was fine, so fine, and I didn't care if I thought he wasn't my type or whatever other bullshit I had said to my Abu and friends before. I just wanted to be with him, even if only for one night.

"Listen, I want it too. I just... I value our friendship. You just told me we're friends, and that means a lot to me. I don't want to mess that up," he whispered, his lips so close to mine I wanted to erase the rest of the space with my longing.

"Trust me, you and me fucking...that won't mess up anything, ok? It would probably be the best decision you ever make. Me for your first time? You'd be in talented hands." I couldn't help myself, my heart hammered inside of me no matter how confident I sounded, and I wanted so desperately to taste his lips.

"Fuck yeah, you're making me change my mind," he said before our lips collided in a frenzy of passion. He tasted like lemons and honey, and I wondered what he'd had to drink before I arrived. Then I forgot all about that as Emile showed me he might not have any experience fucking, but he certainly had experience kissing.

Air became a high-priced commodity when we finally parted, our breaths mingling in the quiet apartment. And because I couldn't help the tingling all over my body, I asked:

"So, are we still waiting or what?"

CHAPTER

SIX

EMILE

"No waiting."

That's all it took for Keyiara to take charge. She held my hand and tugged me forward; I followed again, making her believe she had the strength to pull me to her heart's desire.

She guided me toward the loft stairs, the view of Williamsburg the backdrop to this haphazard seduction that started with a case of blue balls.

The culprit for my pain ended up being the person that put me out of my misery. All day thoughts of Keyiara back in my apartment, touching me, kneading my muscles had played over and over. And over and over, my body reacted to those thoughts, all the blood leaving my organs to supply the hardness needed to convey how much I wanted Keyiara. But I hadn't thought to take care of my lust; I'd been equally preoccupied with my new assignment, which would take all my attention.

Somehow my consciousness remained engaged on work while my subconscious kept coming up with more scenarios where Keyiara and I fucked until we couldn't walk anymore. And my body kept reacting.

By the time she knocked on my door, I'd realized my mistake, and the heaviness I'd felt most of the day changed to a sharp pulsing pain in my balls. I'd thought of ignoring her, sending her away to avoid further embarrassment, but just the thought of not seeing her again or possibly pissing her off completely made my throat close until I opened the door for her.

After climbing the stairs, Keyiara recognized her mistake, stopping right at the top of the steps, which positioned me one step below her, equalizing our heights. I resisted the urge to bury my face in her curls, the scents of lemon and verbena mingling with the sandalwood she used for my handjob. Her supple ass served as the perfect cushion for my increasing hardness, and I gripped her hips, enjoying the feel of her in my hands.

"I have no idea which one is your room," she confessed, a thread of amusement present in her words.

"The corner one to the right," I replied, not letting go of her until she created distance enough for me to navigate the last step.

We entered my room, and I wondered what she saw. This was my most private space—not even D came in here.

"Wow, I didn't expect this..." She whirled, taking the space in. "Are those movie posters?" she asked as she disentangled her fingers from mine, leaving me to stare behind her as she inspected my charcoal wall with frames of my favorite movies, each one illuminated with a warm amber light sconce.

"Yeah, they're my favorite movies."

"No jodas..." she said in wonder, and I'd lived in the city all my life, so I knew what that meant.

The instinct to take cover, to duck and hide rose from where it always lay dormant, ready to command my attention.

In a flash of brown skin and black curls, she turned to face me again and gave me a gentle smile.

"I adored *Someone Great*," she whispered and approached me gently, taking hold of my hand again. The instinct to cover retreated with her nearness. "But that movie is not like the others." She shook her head.

"Yeah, I know. Were you expecting action movies?" I asked as she took another glimpse of the wall, which had most of the great Black Romance movies of our generation.

"Maybe *The Harder They Fall*, or I don't know... *Get Out*?" She faced me again with a grin. "But instead, I find out you're a romantic."

Thank God for my poker face because right now, the flush that suffused me at her words would be a dead give-away. Her eyes studied me with intent, and I stood taking all her interest in, hoping nothing gave me away. "And this?" she asked as she approached the opposite wall with curiosity.

"Those are sketches, physical representations of some of the software and app ideas I've had through the years."

The thought of having sex with Keyiara was as exhilarating as it was intimidating, but having her here in my domain? It was nerve-wracking.

She found the sketch of a logo for an app that had been percolating in my mind for a few years...

"What's this one about?" She gazed quizzically over her shoulder, turning back to the sketch as if it had her in a trance.

"That's a sketch for an app for introverts looking for activities in their cities."

"Yeah? What would it do differently from other apps?"

"Well, it would have ratings that share the amount of socializing required, noise levels, ability to do the activity on your own, etc. I mean, it would be for anyone, but it would be geared toward people like me."

"People like you?"

"You know what I mean." I shrugged and realized I was still naked. The promise of Keyiara had taken away my self-consciousness, but it was back now. She'd seen me without much clothing nearly every Friday of the past year, but something about walking around her swinging left and right didn't sit well.

I turned around and opened the frosted sliding doors of my closet, grabbed a T-shirt for her, and pulled on sweatpants, instantly feeling more secure.

"Here." I handed her the t-shirt. She stared at it as if it would bite her.

"I don't need a t-shirt. Or do I?" There was a challenge in her tone, her ample chest rising and falling as she narrowed her eyes at me, and I wondered what misstep I'd taken.

"I... No, of course not. I was feeling a little exposed and thought you'd..."

"Oh, mi vida. You aren't exposed, that blessing of yours..." She brandished her hand, gesturing toward my body as if it was a magic wand. "Listen, I'm trying not to objectify you, but you're fine as fuck, Emile. No need to hide yourself from me," she said, dropping the t-shirt I'd given her on the floor.

"What did you think I meant, though? You got upset."

"I didn't get upset." She brushed me off, walking toward the window, which showed the city.

"But you did. You talked about knowing me after this year, but I know you too."

She padded her way to my bed, running her hand on the dark blue comforter before she plopped herself on top, crisscrossing her legs and resting her elbow on her knee so she could hold up her face.

Keyiara sat on my bed wearing that brown bra that was losing the fight to contain her abundance, the sepia skin of her thick thighs glimmering under the vanishing sunlight, her plump belly fully relaxed, and her eyes trained on me. Whatever I did to make this miracle happen, I wanted to know so I could keep doing it over and over again.

"So, are you gonna tell me or what?" I said with a little of her same challenge.

"I thought you wanted me to cover myself because of my fatness, and I was about to walk out that door because I don't do losers that pretend not to like fat women but then slide into our DMs trying to smash."

It took all I had not to rear back in insult. Did she truly believe I was that superficial? Had I ever shown her anything but kindness and gentle interest in everything her?

"Nah, you got me mistaken then. I thought we knew each other, but I guess I need to clarify a few things for you." I got on the other side of the bed and rested myself on my side facing her, mirroring her propped head on my fist. It felt odd being on this side of the bed because she'd sat on mine. But I wouldn't say anything—she looked better than I ever did sitting there.

"I'm not a superficial man. I search for what's inside of you before I even register what your outer shell looks like. I've gotten to know you this entire year, and trust me, I like what I see." I leaned closer to her, pulling one of her curls, stretching it, then letting it bounce back.

"Mhm, alright, good. 'Cause I know I look good, papi. I'm a certified ten, but I know people can be cruel, and I don't subject myself to any of that negativity."

"Can I be honest? I hate the whole 'I'm a ten' business.

That we've reduced physical attraction, which is so subjective, to a grade is... Well, it's fucked up."

Keyiara stared at me, then slid down to match my pose.

"All this time, and you're a romantic. Que vaina." She chuckled, her eyes crinkling in amusement, her belly and breasts jiggling as she leaned into her laugh. Fuck, she was breathtaking. She laughed until her eyes watered, then a seriousness crossed her face, a shadow blocking her light.

"So, listen, this is just... I really like you, but this is just two friends fucking, right?" she asked, then held her breath as she awaited the answer.

Any other day I'd have said no, it took more than friendship for me to get things going, but today, it seemed my body had taken charge, maybe tired of all the waiting, of holding off for the right one, of idolizing an imaginary relationship that didn't exist. And here Keyiara was, offering a night of relaxation, passion, and zero ties, and still, I hesitated.

"It seems he agrees with two friends fucking." She pointed at my crotch, where the physical evidence of how ready I was for this friends-with-benefits arrangement throbbed rock-hard.

"Hold up. I'm down with just friends fucking, but I don't know about just a one-time thing."

"Ohh, greedy, greedy." She smiled and ran her fingers from my shoulder down my biceps until she held my hand. "I'm ok with it being more than one time, more than one day. I just don't know if you and I..."

Damn, that hurt, but I was good at keeping my thoughts hidden, so I just stared, willing her to finish her sentence.

"I sometimes feel like I'm...never mind. I think you and I are mature enough to do this without it getting complicated, right?" she finished, and a cold flash came over me, a warning that I should push back a little, ask more. Understand what exactly she meant. But the opportunity passed when with impressive dexterity, she stretched back with one hand and unsnapped the hook of her bra.

I closed my eyes for a second, willing my body to relax. I'd seen naked women before, but I hadn't understood what it was to be completely enthralled by a woman.

Until today.

I'd seen breasts before. My girl in college, then a few more women who tried to convince me they were the answer to my 'ailment.' But there was nothing wrong with me. There was a name for my feelings, for the reasons just a pair of titties didn't do it for me.

Demisexuality.

In all my years of adulthood, I'd been able to admire women's bodies for the masterpieces they were, but arousal didn't always accompany that admiration. Something more needed to be in play for me to feel lust for someone.

Keyiara, with the simple divestment of her bra, awakened feelings I didn't know I had inside of me. This roaring hunger that threatened to take over my clarity had grown these past months until it became an entity of its own inside of me.

"Fuck, Keyiara, you are...glorious. You are glorious."

"Mmmm, yes, those words are doing it for me." She beamed, then removed her leggings in a sexy shimmy.

"Yellow panties for your saint?" I asked, knowing just enough to be dangerous.

"Oh...you really do pay attention. That's also sexy as fuck."

I wanted to preen at her compliment, but instead, I figured I'd show her what her words did to me. The lack of moisture in my mouth wasn't helping as I licked my lower lip. Then, with my eyes on her, I lifted my hips, hooking my fingers on the elastic band of my sweatpants, this time taking longer to pull them all the way off.

"Anytime you're going to take your clothes off for me, do it just like that," she said, wiping imaginary saliva from her lips.

"You're too much." I chuckled, and she smiled at me even though her eyes dimmed for a second.

"Can I be honest?" I asked, wanting this night to be one that I would always remember. She might just want to remain friends after having sex with me a few times, but I knew I'd never forget Keyiara and how lovely she looked laying on my navy comforter, her hands fluttering over her belly.

"Always, that's all I ever want from you," she whispered, and the weight of those words settled between my shoulders.

"I'm nervous as fuck," I confessed.

"Oh, mi vida." She shuffled on the bed, and the shock of her warm skin against mine was delicious torture. She erased all the space between us, bringing my arm to settle on her waist as she cradled her head on my shoulder, our legs tangled in themselves as if they knew each other from way back, and the scent of chocolate and something else hit me as her breath puffed out. "How about we lay like this until our bodies get used to each other, and your heartbeat slows down from a trillion to at least a billion beats per minute?" she asked.

"Let's do that," I replied and rested my head on her curls, the beats of our hearts trying to match up at the same time as my dick promised to embarrass me in a few minutes.

CHAPTER

SEVEN

EMILE

The sun setting outside altered the tone inside my room. Keyiara's breathing changed, going from a shorter inhale and exhale to deep inhalations. Her warmth became my warmth, and my hands started exploring uncharted territory.

"Will you let me know if something doesn't work for you?" I asked and pressed a kiss on her shoulder, then ran my tongue on the same spot, my lips tingling from the contact with her soft skin. I'd read books where a man would taste the woman, and she'd be sweet, but Keyiara didn't taste like a dessert. Her skin was salty, and her verbena smell saturated me. There was another scent mingling with the scent of my body that I could only imagine was her arousal. I lacked the proper words to describe her aroma until *mouthwatering* blazed in my mind.

"Yeah, you know me, I don't stay quiet." She chuckled and lay on her back, pulling her panties off, the darkness of the room making her skin shimmering velvet.

"Good. I want to know if I'm messing up." I followed her, ghosting my finger down from her collarbone, her heartbeat pressing against me. I trailed down the top of her breast slow, slow, slow until I tweaked her nipple. A cute giggle escaped her, and I circled her nub, needing to hear that sound again.

"Can I?" I asked her, nipping the corner of my bottom lip.

Her eyes shined in the darkness, and I paused to enjoy the beauty of her lying next to me, gifting me this moment. She responded with a nod and a sensual lick of her bottom lip that spurred me to steal a quick taste of her mouth.

Her nipple acted as a beacon I was helpless to follow, my entire body vibrating as I dragged my tongue around her areola, the sharp sound of her inhalation sweet music to my ears. I licked her nipple, my mouth full of her delightful flavor, then sucked the entire area into my mouth, making her buck on the bed.

With sure hands, I caressed her other titty, kneading and plumping her beautiful breast as I continued to suck and lick on her nipple.

"Ohh, this is good, very, very good." Keyiara moaned,

her hand tangling in my hair as she pressed herself against me.

Excitement bolted through me as I feasted on her lushness. I must have gotten overexcited because next thing I knew, Keyiara guided my hand down her belly and parked it between her legs.

Heat. Wetness. Suppleness.

"Tell me what you like," I asked her, stealing another kiss from her parted lips, our tongues tangling as her hand taught my hand how she liked to be touched.

"Right there, there." She breathed against my mouth, and I swooped in to kiss her again, desperate to savor her moans. My dick ached to be touched, its hardness nudging her thigh as our bodies slid against each other.

With her guidance, I circled her clitoris, the pliant nub vibrating underneath my fingers before I glided a finger inside her walls.

"Ahhh..." She pushed her head back and rode my hand. I had no idea what to do with my fingers. I'd read some-where that doing a 'come to me' motion would touch her most sensitive area. I tried to do so, but she immediately froze.

"Uh, what are you doing?"

"I'm trying to massage your G-spot."

"Oh...yeah, no, don't do that, it feels weird," she breathed, so I relaxed my finger, wondering if the tech-nique was wrong or if I'd performed it incorrectly. She didn't explain, just went back to riding my hand and showering kisses all over my face, licking and sucking my neck, making me wish I was inside of her already.

"I don't think I can wait much longer," I confessed, a tinge of embarrassment coloring my words.

"Oh, ok, yeah, just can you add one more finger… yessss…" She hissed when my middle finger joined my index. While I fingered her, she played with herself, stroking and strumming her clit to her liking. "Ok, ok, I'm almost there, come."

This was it; this was our moment. I braced myself over her, my dick heavy between us, laying on the apex of her thighs.

"Are you good?" she asked, a sweet smile peeking.

"Fuck, are you kidding? I'm more than great," I assured her, pressing a kiss on her lips. I could have just done that the whole night, kissed and sipped from Keyiara, letting her use my hands for whatever she wanted. But here she was, offering me even more.

I attempted to line up with her, and my heart faltered when I tried to thrust into her and met with resistance.

"No, not there…" she choked.

The heat of her made me dizzy; the need to be inside of her drove me wild. I again attempted to line up at her entrance, and again, Keyiara ran from my dick when I tried to thrust inside her.

"Not there either. Here." The feel of her hand on my dick felt like a glove of goodness around me. I had to fight the urge to just stroke into her fist.

"Here," she whispered in the quiet of the night as I finally felt myself at her entrance.

"Are you sure you're ok with me not using a condom?" I asked.

"Yeah, go ahead, we're covered." Keyiara ran a palm on my cheek, and before I could register what happened, she surged up, enveloping my dick in the most delicious heat I'd ever felt around my length.

I pressed down, wanting to drive my dick all the way into her snug haven, then again and again, until I realized Keyiara wasn't moaning anymore.

"Wait… Wait, you gotta…slow down." Her words were a splash of cold water, and I shook my head to listen to what she had to say.

"You're just ramming inside of me. You're on the large side; it helps if you take it slow at first."

Slow? How could I? I wanted the sensation of her to be the first and last thing I felt every day. I wanted to take her out on dates, then come back to my apartment and sink into Keyiara. I wanted it all.

"I'll try to go slow," I grunted as I gave her one more hard stroke, helpless to seek the snug feel of her walls.

"That's not slow, Emile." She chastised me, and I attempted to slow down again, but it was as if a machine inside me compelled me to thrust, thrust, thrust. Her walls clenched around me, the sensation unleashing the little restraint I had left as my strokes became erratic. I was panting as I drove into her, trying to leave the last couple of inches out of her to avoid any discomfort.

"Fuck, you feel so... Shit, I... I don't think I can hold it much longer," I warned, feeling as if the train had left the station without checking for passengers. I grunted, weird noises escaping me as I poured my entire self into Keyiara. Her warm hand caressed me up and down as I came inside of her, cradled by her spread legs, her pants melding with my own.

I collapsed on top of her, pressing a kiss on her breasts as I placed my face between them, eyes heavy with sleep as I—

"Oh no, no, you don't. Wake up because you need to redeem yourself."

CHAPTER

EIGHT

KEYIARA

Me and my big mouth.

The moment I told Emile he needed to redeem himself, I felt him stiffen against me. I didn't mean to hurt his feelings and missed his warmth as he detached from me and got out of his bed in search of clean underwear.

When he returned to the bed wearing boxer briefs, he stared, then lay back down next to me, but the space between us might as well be the Caribbean Sea.

"You asked me to be honest," I reminded him, again not knowing when to stop.

"Yeah, I did."

"So why are you being like this now?"

"How am I being?" He inquired so politely I felt like bopping him in the head to make him snap out of it.

59

"Like you're upset I was honest."

"I'm not upset."

"Really?" I rolled over closer to him, and his breath hitched. "See!"

"I don't know what you—"

"If you say you don't know what I mean, I will pinch you."

"Remind me again how old you are?"

I wanted to scream and laugh at the same time. This façade he could wear sometimes had no place between us in this bed tonight. If it killed me, I'd make sure this night would be memorable for him, not because of his luke-warm first performance but because we tried and tried again until it felt amazing for both of us. The tingling in my fingers had never failed me.

"I think you've been wanting to ask that question for a long time. How old do you think I am?" I asked him curiously.

"Based on everything you've told me about you, you're probably thirty-one," he replied.

"Were you out here calculating my date of birth or what?"

"So, I'm right?" he asked, a drop of smugness in his tone.

"Yeah, yeah," I grumbled. "So, are you gonna tell me why you're mad?"

"I'm not..." He pushed up, resting his back against the headboard, clearly exasperated with my line of questioning.

"I wanted you to enjoy it as much as I enjoyed it." He shrugged. I was losing him to his aloofness and the wall he could erect so expertly around himself.

"Alright then, let's try again. This night hasn't ended," I reminded him, unwilling to lie. If this man walked away from this bed thinking what he did was a good performance... Nah, my sisterhood—*I* deserved better.

"Mmm, but what if..." He pressed his lips shut and shook his head.

"What if? If this is it? Boy, if I was graded by my original performance my first time, I'd be tabled a pillow princess. And that's not who I am," I rushed to say when I saw his eyebrow lift as if he had doubts about my assertions.

"I'm gonna ignore that look you just gave me," I said and jumped off the bed, strolling over to his closet, where I took one of his hoodies and pulled it on before I rummaged around and found a pair of basketball shorts that appeared my size.

Then once I did that, I left the room.

"Keyiara?" I heard him ask.

"Where you going?" he asked again, his tone shifting. He was still in shutdown mode.

"I'll be right back!" I hollered back and rushed to find my bag and my cell phone. After checking I had no missed calls, I brought my things back to his room with me.

I walked in to find him pacing by his bed, but the moment he felt my presence, he plunked back on the mattress.

"Nah, get up. I want to dance bachata."

"Dance?"

"Yeah, I know you're not about to tell me you don't know how to dance some bachata. I'm sure you had a little Afro-Dominican or Afro-Puerto Rican shorty in high school." I extended my hand to him, beckoning closer.

The skepticism oozed from every pore in his body, but even with all of that, he came to me. I resisted the urge to crow in triumph, knowing that even though he worked on erecting his walls, he still responded to my call.

"She was Panamanian," he murmured, and now it was my turn to raise my eyebrows.

I tapped my screen and quickly found the song I wanted to play.

Romeo Santos crooned in our ears. The first eight notes were enough for my hips to undulate to the strains of the accordion as the familiar tune began its first words. Emile stood still in the middle of his room while I advanced toward him. The fabric of the hoodie I was planning to steal brushed against his abs, and then the front of my body molded into him. All along, my hips swung their syncopated rhythm, my feet doing what they were born to do. Eyes closed, I let the sway of my body lure Emile until the heat of his hand grazed my waist, and he pulled me flush against him. And just as I suspected, he matched my rhythm, clearly familiar with the steps to take.

"Is he singing about cheating?" Emile whispered in my ear.

"Yeah, he's making an indecent proposal," I responded back. My skin tightened as our gazes connected, his deep brown eyes mesmerizing in the moonlight.

"And this is what you thought to play to dance with me?" he said, the reproof clear.

"It's one of my favorite songs from him." I couldn't have possibly played the other one. That would have been... Nah, he knew too much Spanish. It would reveal too much.

"Mhm, what are the other ones?"

"Do you know Romeo Santos's songs?"

"No, but still, I'm curious."

"Tell me where you learned to dance, and I will tell you."

"I learned to dance bachata with my ex-girlfriend. The Panamanian."

"Mhm, she taught you well," I said, ignoring the cramp in my stomach at the mention of his ex-girlfriend. "See how you matched my movements at the beginning, then you took over and guided me? See how I've let my body go with the flow, and you've matched the same energy?" I whispered as Romeo asked his lady what would happen if he lifted her skirt.

"Yeah." He guided me to a two-step where our hips rolled from side to side, then front to back. Damn. Where was all of this when we were fucking earlier?

"See what you just did there? You matched the energy, then added a little bit more, enough to make things even better? That game of give and take, the trust that I will follow where you lead, that connection between our bodies? That's what was missing between us," I explained, hoping I wouldn't lose him to his stoicism.

"Our interop was all off," Emile said in awe, and I knew he was doing some of his coding talk.

"Interop?"

"Interoperability. Basically, it allows different systems to talk and comprehend information passed to each other."

"Yep, talk sexier to me, papi," I responded because goddamn, I loved it when he went all sexy nerd on me.

"Here you go." He chuckled, the vibrations rumbling deep inside of me. His proximity, the smell of sandalwood, and the sensual feel of his body against mine all made me wish for more than just this night.

"Kiss me, Emile."

He stared down at me with a grin and realized I was serious. The grin converted into that lip bite, and he moved down as if hypnotized until his lips caressed mine. His tongue ventured inside my mouth, and again he gave me a master class in kissing. The dance move he'd just pulled was child's play compared to the sensations he created inside of me. One kiss turned into two, then more as he ushered me to the bed, the soft mattress stopping me short till we fell together.

The urge to let him take me now was essential, but I knew he still felt raw. I felt him tense as I rubbed myself against him as if I was in heat, pulling him flush on top of me, his head nestling in my cleavage, his hands tugging at my clothes in a frenzy.

"Remember, interop." Then I licked his earlobe.

"Fuck, Keyiara, you really trying to make me laugh right now?" We both shook in amusement.

"Yep, that's also interop too."

CHAPTER

NINE

KEYIARA

Skin-to-skin contact was always a pleasurable experience for me. It replenished my tank; it was such an intimate gesture for me. Skin-to-skin contact with Emile could be one of the best experiences of my life. Every particle in my body glowed in response as his chest pressed against mine, our bodies aligned, seeking solace from each other.

In a brilliant move, Emile flipped us, making me feel like a feather as he maneuvered me on top of him. His hands roamed all over my heated skin as I guided him in. We both groaned when he slid inside, the feel of his dick making me believe Anaisa had sent him just for me.

I rose up, luxuriant in my search for ecstasy, clenching my inner walls around his thick girth.

"Fuck, that's...is your pussy magical?" he mumbled,

teasing a smile out of me as I continued to ride him, seeking both of our orgasms.

Bouncing on his dick, I gave him some of my 'all rings will be closed' magic, sweat trickling down my back as I put in the work that my watch would praise me for later. Every time he moaned, I swirled to make him do it one more time, every time he clenched his hands on my hips, I pulsed my walls around him, and every time he reached out to tweak my nipples, I gushed on him.

The tendons on his neck flexed and tensed as he pressed his head back on his pillow, his mouth open in a silent scream as he started matching me stroke for stroke. With impressive strength, he held onto my hips, then pounded inside of me, starting a quake I didn't think would be possible on his second time.

"Oh my god, you feel so fucking tight and wet, and how do you do that with your...fuck!" He pushed up and did something with his dick that was exactly what my pussy needed, proving he was a fast learner and I was a fantastic teacher. My fingers twitched as the pressure built, then released, my entire body floating as I reached my climax.

One more thrust and Emile froze under me, the delicious feel of his dick expanding and throbbing inside of me enough to make my fingers twitch again.

"See, that paid off." I sighed into his chest, then tried to roll over to the bed, only to be stopped in my forward movement.

"Nah, don't move yet. You're mad comfy," he said,

again making me feel as light as a feather, now with his words.

I shrugged and nestled into him, enjoying the feel of his softening penis inside of me. Unfortunately, nature intruded, and I hastily disentangled myself from him, promising to be back shortly when he grumbled his protest.

A quick rinse of my body in his shower had me good as new. I rummaged around in his bathroom and found a washcloth, which I brought out for him.

The expected soft snores were absent. Instead, a wide-awake Emile trailed my approach to his bed, my eyes quickly adjusting back to the darkness of his room.

I gently wiped his dick, then tossed the washcloth to the floor.

"When you do this with other women, make sure to get them something to clean up with if you dick them down good," I recommended, only to receive a loud scoff from him.

"I'm not doing this with you to learn tips for other women." The decisive statement had an odd effect on me —the same tingling in my fingers returned, and I felt suspended on air, high in the sky. Brushing off the feeling, I pretended not to understand.

"I'm sure you don't, but the advice stands." I shrugged, shimming my way into his side, his warmth a magnet to my now-cool skin.

"Damn, you're cold. Why did you have to take a

shower and chase away that hot goodness you had going on?" he asked, disgruntled. This groucho.

"Why are you so moody sometimes?" I asked, tickled by his grunt as I planted my feet in between his legs.

"I'm not moody, not really. I'm just easily overstimulated," he explained, and a lot of things started to make sense with that simple reply.

"Huh, that makes sense. My father is a little like that too. He can hang out at parties and stuff and does it for my Mai and me, but he prefers to just be home, chilling in his quiet apartment. It's where he is the happiest."

"I can relate," he said and pressed me closer, draping an arm around me. "How's he, by the way? Still trying to win your moms back?" he asked, fully aware of my parents' story. They were childhood sweethearts that married young, still inexperienced. Five years ago, Daddy decided he wanted to leave Mai. He said they had become roommates instead of lovers. A year later, he was trying to convince her to move back in with him. She refused. Ever since, he'd been relentlessly courting her.

"Yeah, he comes by to the restaurant every morning before going to work, and at every Rodriguez clan party, he's there. Mai acts like she's unbothered, but the other day Abu called me, and Mai hadn't slept at home." I chuckled, enjoying the rumble of his laughter.

"Good for him. If your mom is like you, I get why he's fighting so hard to get her back." My pulse fluttered at his words, and I tried to make things lighter.

"Charmer, you just trying to get in my pants."

"I hate to break it to you, but that already happened." He harrumphed when I punched his stomach.

We relaxed into the silence of the room, the stillness of the early evening lulling us both to drowsiness. Something had been nagging me for a minute, and I couldn't fall asleep until I asked.

"Can I ask you something?"

"Anything," he responded, making my eyes close in satisfaction.

"Why were you still... Why hadn't you had sex with someone yet?"

"I knew this was coming," he said placidly. "I had one girlfriend throughout high school and through college. And we were supposed to have our first time together. It was the first time I had fallen in love. I knew I was different than my boys, you know? I mean, they were horny all the fucking time, whereas I...not until Yamilah. Once I fell for her, I got why my friends were so horny.

"So yeah, we'd talked about it, built the whole thing up in our heads. Then I found out from my brother, of all people, that Yamilah had been smashing one of the boys in her college. I was at NYU, and she was going to CUNY. That shit devastated me. Took me a while to get my confidence back."

My heart constricted at his story; how could she do something like that to him? You could tell that inside his stoic façade was a very sensitive man. If I ever bumped into that Yamilah, she'd get a meet and greet with my fists. But that only accounted for his young adulthood—many years had passed since then, I couldn't keep from asking.

"Yeah, I know. It's been interesting for me. I meet women; I've told you of dates I've been on. I jive with some but never at a deep level. I know part of it is me. I keep myself very closed off at the beginning, but it's hard to open up. Daymond says our father programmed me like a robot, and I never broke through like him."

"Daymond can catch these fists," I grumbled.

"Nah, he's partially right. Daymond saw our father as a man the moment he became a teenager, but I still saw him as a deity, so I didn't see where his advice was flawed. I just acted like he told me to act. That used to work with women before, the strong, silent type. Now women want an equal partner that can emote. And...it's hard for me to get from point A to point B."

"Mhm, ok... So you go on dates, but they never get to crack the code?"

"Yeah, maybe, or maybe I don't give myself enough space to let them crack the code. I've had some people I've seen for months, and they know I'm demisexual, but...it gets old after a while for them."

There it was—something I knew and understood about him but that he hadn't put into so many words. I knew it took him a while to get there because he needed to feel a connection; it all made sense to me. But what did that mean about us?

I wanted to ask him what had changed, but I wasn't ready for truth-telling tonight. So instead, I snuggled into him.

"Well, I'm happy it was me who had the honor."

"Me too, Keyiara. Me too."

TEN

KEYIARA

"So, are you gonna let me see it up close or what?"

If someone had told me I'd be waking up next to Emile Walker after a night of three rounds of raising-the-spirits finger-tingling sex, I'd have asked when exactly it was happening and made sure I rested the night before to get ready for the mind-blowing experience. However, if someone had told me Emile would ask to see my pussy so he could learn me... Well, that would have knocked me out my seat.

That first time had been a fluke; each time after that, Emile had applied himself to pleasing every inch of my body while he also touched my soul. He still had that new feeling to him, like every move and sensation was a roller-coaster ride, but that made the experience even more endearing. But this latest ask had me ready to blush.

"Emile, no," I whined, tickled by the pout he gave me. His white sheets draped over his back as he rested his folded arms and face on my belly, his warm body nudged between my thighs. We'd just finished our 'let's take care of that morning wood' round, and Emile looked pleased with himself. As he should be—he'd make me come twice in ten minutes. Some of it felt like luck, but I'd take it.

"I just want to learn you better." He pressed his face to my belly, giving me a buzz.

"Oye! Stop, that's ticklish!"

"Ok, I'll stop if you let me see," he promised.

I didn't know why I was acting shy all of a sudden. There wasn't a shy bone in my body, but something about having Emile between my legs, studying me, made my heart flutter and other things throb.

"Ok, but... Just be serious, ok?"

"I'm always serious." His voice was muffled as he slid his body down the bed to better position himself to view the apex of my legs. Impatiently, he yanked the sheets off both of us, the morning sun streaming into the room, giving me forgiving lighting at least.

"Mhmmm." I felt that rumble inside of me, the warmth of his breath teasing my entrance. "Yours is bigger than what I've seen."

"What you mean, bigger?" I asked, affronted.

"Bigger is not the right word... Plumper. It's hot as fuck. Just as fine as her owner." Emile delivered this so matter-of-factly you'd think he was chatting about his latest project.

"Ok...yeah, I have a fatty. But every woman's vulva is different, you know this."

"Yeah, I know, but I'm not down here to look at your vulva because of that. I'm here to learn you."

My stomach did a lazy jaunt down my body, and the tingle...

"So, what else do you want to learn?" I asked, my breath coming a bit airy, the shyness from before transforming to anticipation.

"Well, I was thinking I'd love to learn how to touch you...to lick you, to make you orgasm for me."

"Oh..."

The press of his mouth right on my pussy lips felt like the first touch of chocolate cake on my tongue. Soft, velvety, delicious goodness.

Just when I thought Emile couldn't surprise me anymore, the tip of his tongue flicked my hidden nub, teasing it out of its hiding place.

"Oh, Emile, what...are you..." He attempted to suck my clit into his mouth, but the pressure increased too quickly for me.

"Hold on...slow down. My clit is...sensitive, I don't like direct pressure like that," I advised, and immediately he took the note, lightening the pressure. Taking his time, he licked and kissed all around my labia and the edges of my thighs, teasing the entrance of my vagina.

"Ohh yes, right, you can slip it in."

The feel of his tongue inside me made me worry I'd drown him with my pleasure.

"Stay still. I'm here trying to master this, and your moans, and your taste, and your wetness... I'm gonna come again just eating you out," he warned me.

No fanfare, just Emile telling me how much he loved eating me out.

"I can't stay still while you tease me like that with your tongue, I need more."

He dragged his tongue up in slow motion till he found my clit again, this time giving it the right pressure. Then, just when I couldn't take it any longer, he inserted two fingers in one slick glide.

"Ahh..."

"I won't be fumbling trying to find your entrance anymore," he stopped to promise, then applied himself to his lesson.

The pressure he created built under the morning sun, the rays attempting to fight the creeping coldness that signaled the season was truly here. I fisted the white sheets when, with luxurious swipes of his tongue while pumping me with his fingers, Emile brought me to my third orgasm of the morning, my whole body quivering in ecstasy.

"So, what's this again?"

"Tres golpes. Are you really telling me you've never had Dominican breakfast?" I put my fist on my hip, pointing to Emile with his wooden spoon. After taking a shower together, my growling stomach forced us to take a break to recharge our bodies. Raiding Emile's fridge, I'd put together the best approximation of fried salami, fried cheese, eggs, and mangu. He'd surprised me with plantains, explaining he'd fallen in love with them after the famous girlfriend.

"Nah, I've had mangu, though. Yours is the best one I've tried."

"Charmer," I cooed, then attacked my plate, still standing against his kitchen island. We ate in companionable silence, and I could sense Emile's happiness. This was his element. He was totally at ease in his sweatpants, no shirt, enjoying the quiet of the morning, the coldness of the floor underneath our feet, the warm, delicious food in our bellies. The taste of the mangu dissolved in my mouth, and not for nothing, I really had done a bomb job with breakfast.

"Food after sex hits different," he confessed, running his tongue across his bottom lip to catch any stray crumbs.

"Yes, it does. I love that I get to spend this first with you."

"I love it too."

"So...about yesterday. You were telling me you're demi, right, and I was wondering why now? Why me?" That question had been circling around my mind for a while, and I'd gone to bed thinking I didn't want answers, but I had been playing games with myself.

The clank of his fork on the plate made me look up, and our eyes connected, lingering until all the hairs on my body rose up. With the intensity between us, I had to empty my lungs to cut some of the tension. And the tingling in my fingers... I couldn't deny that my instinct, my heart, and Anaisa were all trying to shout at me.

"Are you ready for me to answer that?" Those deep brown eyes of his nudged at me, testing my resolve. I severed the eye contact, feeling empty the moment my gaze trailed down to my plate.

"So...what do you do on Saturdays, and do I fit into that plan?"

"Are you staying the day?" His hopeful tone made my stomach take a deep dive into the pool of optimism.

"Why not? I mean, we're still in the exploration phase, aren't we? I'm down to hang out," I said, completely rearranging my weekend plans; some voice inside told me this was the thing to do. My instinct told me to take the plunge, but could I trust myself?

I didn't know if this was the right thing to do, but I wasn't looking for right, I was looking for now. And if I kept saying that to myself, maybe it would become true.

CHAPTER

ELEVEN

EMILE

We cleaned the kitchen together, despite my insistence that I should do it on my own as Keyiara made breakfast. Her adorable frown, accompanied by pursed lips, was enough signal to give up the fight and let her help to her heart's content.

"So, have you kept at your weed love bites?" I finished scrubbing the pan she'd used to fry the salami, handing it to her for rinsing.

"Yeah, you know I bake at least once a week."

"And still, you don't bring me any." I shook my head, the last dish in the sink clean, avoiding eye contact. I'd been hearing about these Kiki cannabis bites for eight months, and for eight months, she'd kept me waiting. Other friends and family had tried the bites, so the message was clear. I turned around and followed her with my eyes.

The sight of Keyiara walking around straightening things in my home in my basketball shorts and hoodie ignited something long lost inside of me.

Hope.

She came into my life a year ago, and since then, I'd let myself fall slowly but irrevocably in awe of her. It had been the most natural way to sink into love. And sink it was because I never expected her to reciprocate. Having her like this…it was heady. A once-in-a-lifetime moment I meant to enjoy until she decided this wasn't for her.

In so many ways, she'd told me she didn't feel I was her type. This morning was no exception. During conversations about her different dates, her joking about how stoic I was, how she'd probably drive me wild with all her talking…all these little ways to let me know what she thought of our compatibility. Even yesterday, she made a point of explaining this was a friendly gesture, the breathtaking Amazon giving her introverted client a taste of magic. And I must be a damn fool because I ran to accept her gift. I wouldn't do it any other way. So, knowing she didn't want me to taste her bites yet because I wasn't in her inner circle wasn't something I wanted to dwell on.

"You know I'll bring some as soon as they are perfect." She smirked, then went over to the living area, dropping to the sofa with a contented sigh.

"Alright." I shrugged, pushing away the usual disappointment, and followed her path to the sofa. I pulled a laptop from the drawer of the coffee table, firing it up to check my emails.

"No, señor. You're not about to work while I'm here, sir." The warm weight of her breasts and belly pressed against my side as Keyiara attempted to snap the laptop closed. I wasn't surprised by her gesture, but I was surprised I didn't feel a trace of annoyance at her insistence.

"I just need to send one email to my new client." I dropped a kiss on her shoulder, then turned back to the laptop. She froze next to me, the jerk of tension in her body making me focus on her face again. Her gaze, full of wonder and tenderness, nearly knocked me out my seat.

"That was sweet." Her brown cheeks bloomed to a darker shade as she fought away her blush.

"You're sweet." Her parted lips were all the invitation I needed to taste her. The lingering taste of the sweet coffee and milk she had with breakfast had me sliding and licking, wanting to get at the core of her.

"You're also so good at that." Her lips curved into a smile against mine, and I leaned in to explore if the taste of her smile would be different than her taste of tenderness.

The variables were similar, but there was a slightly different feel to this kiss, and I reveled in it. The kiss consumed me, and I scrambled to drop the laptop off my lap. The only reasonable thing to do after that was to get Keyiara's sumptuous weight on me and explore her to my heart's content.

"Oh, oh, so sorry I was just being a brat earlier, but if you need to do one of your integrate... What's it called, integration testing? I understand." She continued pressing high-inducing kisses to my mouth, chin, and neck, almost making me miss the fact she remembered the name of the previous client's job.

"Nah, this new client..." The drag of her tongue against my Adam's apple momentarily made me lose my train of thought.

"Your new client?" She giggled, then nibbled my earlobe, running her tongue around my earring.

"Yeah...uh. My new client, this job is a penetration testing job."

"A what?" She reared back, her eyes shining with amusement.

"You're a perv."

"You too, if you know where my mind went." The giggles intensified, making her ass and hips jiggle on my lap, which, in turn, made other things intensify.

"Penetration testing is when you check the vulnerabilities of a system. Basically, you run code to attempt to bring to light any breaches in the software."

Her eyes clouded, then her face underwent a myriad of rapid changes, none of the thoughts in her brain rooted enough for me to read her expressions.

"So, like, purposely hacking a system?"

"Yeah, something like that..."

"Huh." She wiggled on my lap, and my dick rose to the

occasion, wanting to feel those wiggles till I came all inside of her.

"Ahh, Keyiara...if you keep doing that..."

"What? I was just thinking, isn't what we're doing together a bit like penetration testing? Us fucking so you can see all the variables and make sure we check your sexual vulnerabilities?" She smirked when I pressed my fingers into her pliable hips to stop all movement. I thought of what she said and understood why she had come to that hilarious conclusion, but there was no testing happening on my side. I wouldn't bother saying that, though. This weekend was too perfect for me to bring any type of feelings to this conversation.

"I guess you could say that."

"Huh." She shifted again, and that was one shift too many. I flipped her off my lap and plopped her onto the sofa. Her laughter trickled inside me, the answer to all my internal coding.

"See? That was a test! You can't last too long with me on your lap." She cackled as I pulled my sweatpants off and yanked my basketball shorts off her plump legs. I pinned Keyiara down, the magic of her lushness making all my blood rush down to my penis. Our gazes connected, hers full of humor and lust, mine shuttered because I couldn't show her all I was feeling.

"Ok, let's test this. Let's test who comes first. And let me tell you, I'm an expert in perseverance," I said. The sensation of wetness surrounding me was still so new I had to pause to collect myself. But Keyiara didn't play fair.

The squeeze of her walls on my dick would have been enough to fire my engine, but the drag of her tongue on my nipple had me fighting to keep my head in the game.

Fuck the test. I just wanted to sink into her and get lost.

I attempted to bring finesse to my strokes, timing my movements to the flutters and squeezes of Keyiara's pussy. I let her moans be the guiding light to my own orgasm. I now understood what she'd meant about my size, so I kept that in mind. My consideration paid off, her velvety wetness even snugger but with a yield that I didn't experience the first night.

"So, are you gonna fold? Come for me, Keyiara."

"If you call me Kiki, I'll come all over this dick." She moaned in my ear, and her filthy mouth would probably have me folding first.

"Come for me, Kiki," I whispered, the feelings of the day saturating every syllable.

And as if I had pushed a button, Keyiara quivered, a long string of Spanish words spilling out of her mouth as she took me right with her.

"So, if you want me to melt into a puddle, call me Kiki. When you say my name, it sounds indecent," she confessed as she nestled on top of me. We were still on my large sofa as Keyiara surfed my different streaming services, searching for the right thing to watch. I didn't care what she played; I only knew I wanted to stay here, under her.

She navigated until she found where I'd left off with *The Photograph.*

"You were watching this?" I tensed under her, wondering if there was censure in her tone.

"Yeah, it's one of my favorite current romance movies." I shifted, making us both comfortable as she nestled her lower body between my legs.

"Right, the posters."

"Yeah, romance movies are my favorite. Not something I could watch easily at home with my dad." Somehow with her, this wasn't something to hide or be embarrassed about. It felt good to share this aspect of myself, to open up to her. Over the years, some of my father's antiquated views had tainted mine of masculinity and what it meant to be a Black man.

The definition of that, according to my father, was to be stoic, introspective. It meant to protect and to keep your thoughts inside. It meant being solid and dependable. The thing was before people got to know me, they only saw that outer image I portrayed, the one that had been drilled into my mind all my childhood. But Keyiara, without trying, had chipped away at that outer layer and made a space for herself.

"Mhm, if I ever meet that father of yours... I'm not much of a romance girly, I like cozy mysteries better, but I'm always down to watch romance movies with you." Her words, simple and unassuming, were exactly what I needed to hear. She might fight our attraction and focus on our differences, but this was how it could be if only she let me in.

"So I got to tell you...sometimes I jack off to my favorite scenes in romance movies. I'd done that before that session I ended up bricked up," I confessed, throwing it all in. If this was the only time she'd give me, I wanted her to really know me.

"Emile!" she gasped, then her laughter took over her entire body, the shaking making me grin.

"You good?" I asked her when she finally paused enough to catch her breath.

"Oh, I'm real good. I just realized you showed me your porn wall last night," Keyiara said before bursting into laughter again, the sound of her filling me with joy.

CHAPTER

TWELVE

KEYIARA

This was the second night together, so I'm not sure how I'd missed that Emile snored. It wasn't a snore; it was more of a weird vibration against my back, but it was insistent enough to wake me up from my deep slumber. I scrunched up my eyes, hoping I'd fall asleep again.

Last night we watched a new romance movie, then we took a stroll around his neighborhood, ending up at his corner bodega, where we stocked up on snacks and a few groceries for breakfast this morning. It had all flowed so well, so easy; it felt like the perfect non-planned date. We popped popcorn and played Battleship, we listened to music—all things right up his alley.

The best chill night.

Then when the night settled into full darkness, we had slow, easy sex. The kind where you laugh and pause to talk and then start again. The kind that had no rush because the goal wasn't to orgasm but to enjoy each other's bodies. The kind that made your heart tremble and your soul shiver.

I was running out of reasons why this man wasn't perfect for me. But the snoring was a good starting point.

"Yo! Wake up, you're mad loud." I pushed my elbow back, not even eliciting a grunt from Emile.

"It's not me. It's your cell phone. Someone is trying to locate you." The tickle of his breath on my ear made me sigh in contentment. His warm hands caressed my back until a hard surface touched my skin, sliding up my waist until it landed next to my belly.

Ohh, yeah, I missed I had left my phone on the bed.

Damn, who was so pressed?

The screen lit up the otherwise dark room. We'd closed Emile's blackout curtains, planning on a late wakeup, which he only did on Sundays. I hated to tell him I used my blackouts every day, but that wasn't something I needed to share yet.

Rubbing my eyes for a better view, I saw the many notifications on my phone from my friends, ending with Juju's last attempt to reach me mere minutes ago.

Juju: Kiki, why aren't you answering, are we doing brunch or what? I got the table for 12:30. It's eleven. Chop chop chica!

Brunch! We'd been planning this for weeks. Juju had reserved a table for eight in Angels of Harlem, a spot we loved because of its delicious food, amazing atmosphere, and the crowd that frequented the spot. I'd been looking forward to our boozy Sunday brunch, but could I really trade that for the warmth of Emile's bed and his fine, fine company?

"You went quiet on me, but I can still hear each thought bouncing around your head. You're a loud thinker."

"Nah, just reading these texts."

Emile's arm snaked around my waist, and he brought me closer, his chest the perfect support against my bare back. With a sure hand, he trailed my belly upward till he cradled one of my breasts, massaging the mound, then tweaking my nipple.

"And what made you tense?" The pull of his fingers on my nub made the rest of my body wake up to the allure of Emile.

"I forgot I had brunch with my friends today."

"And you want to go?" I heard the slight hope for no.

I was the girl that wanted to chill with her loud-ass friends in a loud restaurant on Sundays because it was fun, and I enjoyed their company. I didn't know if our lifestyles fit together, no matter how natural it was between us and how we'd gotten to understand each other.

"I do," was my simple reply.

"Ok, then, let's get a shower." He flicked my nipple again, the throbbing between my legs intensifying. I rubbed my legs together and pressed my ass against his morning wood. If we hurried, we still had time.

"I mean, we still have a little time..."

"What time is the reservation?"

"At 12:30 p.m."

"Do you have something to wear?" he asked curiously.

"Yeah, I actually always have a change of clothes in my backpack. Never know where the day will take me."

"So, we have how long to get where exactly?"

"Harlem," I told him reluctantly.

"So, half an hour to get ready, an hour to get there on the train..." A sharp sting on my ass made me jump away from his dick, the pain radiating through me.

"Carajo! Why you slap me for?"

"To get you going. Let's take a shower." He chuckled, then sat up, stretching his arms over his head, all the wonderful smooth skin teasing me. With sure movements, he rose from the bed, his dick bouncing as he sauntered to his bathroom.

I massaged my tender ass cheek, then followed him, grumbling all the way.

"I CAN'T BELIEVE I let you convince me we had time to fuck," I complained in a whisper as I sat in the Uber, squirming to combat the wetness between my legs.

"So that's what happened when you cornered me against my door and told me you wouldn't let me out until I gave you some?" he drawled, staring at me unperturbed.

"Shhh. Whatever." I dismissed his attempt to be accurate and rational. "All I know is, the moment I showed you I had no panties on under my dress, you pressed me against that door and..."

He chuckled, then reached across the car, leaning until his mouth hovered over my ear. "And I fucked you until you begged me to let you come."

"Wow, you let negroes in, and they think they're pipe slingers," I grumbled, and he shut me up with a soft press of his lips on mine. I slid my tongue out to meet his, but he left me kissing the air, relaxing back to his side of the car.

"We're in the Uber, I need you to behave now." He winked, and I swear if it wasn't for the homegirl in front driving, I would have bopped him already. I confirmed that when I heard her giggle in response to his comment.

"We're here," she announced cheerily, giving me a wide-eyed eyebrow wiggle when we made eye contact.

We exited the Uber, saying our thanks as the bass of the music filtered out of the restaurant to us. The spot was already booming, people milling around and sitting at the bar and their tables, dancing and chatting. They were playing some dancehall, and I turned to Emile, worried this might be too much.

"You good?" I held his hand, and he squeezed it, nodding.

"Girl! I thought you were going to ghost us." Juju

greeted us with a smile and a hug. Ephraim, her brother, trailed behind, and Lira stood next to him, waiting to greet us as well.

"Who else is all there?" I asked Juju as we walked to our already occupied table.

"Daymond came through with his new lady, and Ephraim brought Marsh."

Fuck. Marsh was Ephraim's best friend, but the man was the definition of annoying. He thought he was hot shit and acted like all of us were beneath him because he lived in Manhattan and was a lawyer. Daymond, the actual one that was the wealthiest of all of us, was super down to earth and never ever flaunted his work or status.

Ephraim knew that Marsh was an asshole but stuck with him because Marsh had been there for Ephraim and Juju through some tough times, helping them with some legal issues. So even though he also got on Ephraim's nerves, he didn't stop inviting him to shit.

"What? My brother, out for brunch on a Sunday? Ok, I see how it is!" Daymond exclaimed when he saw Emile. Emile gave him a one-armed hug, not letting go of me. Daymond's curious glance at our interlaced hands told me he had many questions but knew his brother enough not to interrogate him here.

"Yo! Y'all made it. I was wondering if you were gone stand us up! I mean, I was planning to buy everyone this first round, so I didn't want you to miss out," Marsh's annoying voice declared. He was so *obnoxious*.

I closed my eyes, hoping things would flow well today. The loud music, Marsh, and the crowd all threatened to be the perfect mix for overstimulation. And what would happen if Emile just couldn't hang?

THIRTEEN

EMILE

The clink of silverware on china repeatedly drilled a hole in my head. Loud laughter boomed around the table as everyone fought to make themselves heard, making my teeth ache. The DJ clearly felt threatened by the hum of conversation because he cranked up the volume. The fast pace of the music accelerated the beat of my heart.

Deep breaths. I could handle this. This was nothing new for me, I had been in loud places before. I needed to retreat into my head and dim the noise. Clear my mind and hope for time to speed until I could feel the cool fall air on my face. Feel my pulse slow as I strolled away from the clamoring.

The caress of Keyiara's fingers against my sweating palm soothed me. The soothing was the equivalent of throwing a bucket of water into a burning inferno—helpful but not nearly sufficient to calm me down. But the gesture... It illuminated a corner inside, that corner that glowed brighter and brighter at the possibilities with Keyiara. She smiled and winked at me, then turned around, her entire face and body alive as she chatted with Ephraim. Her laugh, so distinct, ran melodiously through me compared to the other noises.

"Listen, dude, you should see the amount of cash I'm raking in through my stocks. Fucking wild, son! Listen, son, you need to invest—I can let you know what stocks if you need help." Marsh, who was clearly full of shit and full of himself. Spittle hit my arm as he gesticulated, and my skin crawled.

Why did I come here with Keyiara?

I knew why—I wanted to be with her. Anywhere she was, that's where I wanted to be. But this noise, the pounding of my heart, the radiating pain in my head, and the hollowness in my stomach, were all testing my resolve. I turned around and caught her shimmying in her seat, beaming as she swayed to the rhythm of the music.

Unexpectedly, an intense rush of annoyance spread through me. Marsh poked my arm, the press against my bicep making me wish I could break that finger.

"You don't want me to hook you up?" he asked, his expression completely oblivious to my aggravation.

"No," I drawled.

Daymond smothered a laugh, his gaze of commiseration not helping at all.

The skin of my face tightened as the DJ started playing a Beyoncé song. The noise before? Child's play. The music amplified across the space as people rose up in their seats to chant at the top of their lungs. Pressure pounded behind my eyes.

"Are you alright?" Keyiara's soft whisper boomed into my ear, her attempts to keep her voice low not enough to counteract it all. The thumping of my heart increased, and cold sweat trickled down my back, and still, on the other side of me...

"Listen, man, you're missing out. I told Ephraim I'd hook him up too. You know, I should start some classes..." I tuned him out, tired of his bullshit. Undeterred by my cold shoulder, Marsh turned around to Juju and kept talking, switching to some other asinine topic.

The clapping and hollering amplified, and when the DJ talked over the music, my chest contracted, my hands growing clammy until I couldn't take it anymore. Disentangling my fingers from Keyiara's, I pushed my seat back, the scratch of the chair raking through my dwindling patience.

The door never felt farther away as I fought patrons as they laughed and sang in my face, everyone so happy while the air around me grew thinner.

A few more steps...

"Emile," Daymond called from behind me, but I didn't bother turning around. There was no reason; he knew what was happening.

"Emile."

I didn't stop until I crossed the entrance, the crisp air a relief.

"Bruh, you good?"

I stared at Daymond, not bothering to answer.

"It hasn't got this bad in a while?"

"Yeah. I'm usually good at the coping mechanisms I learned in therapy, but I don't know, man, today was just bad. It didn't help to be seated next to that..." I waved toward the restaurant.

"I know. So you're gonna try to go back in?"

Just the thought of walking back in there made my entire body freeze.

"Nah."

"Aw, man. Ok. Are you gonna let Kiki know, though? Y'all rode together."

I didn't want to leave Keyiara behind, but I knew she'd prefer to stay with her friends. She'd been so eager to come, and I didn't want to ruin her Sunday flow.

"She's having a blast, let her stay. We'll link up later. Let her know I'll hit up her phone."

I walked away, secure knowing that Keyiara would understand.

FOURTEEN

KEYIARA

"Excuse me, he said what?" I couldn't have heard Daymond correctly. I clearly understood wrong. It must be the noise.

"Emile had to split. He...he needed a break. He said to hit him up when you were done here."

The same noise that drove him away without an explanation swirled around me. I'd been feeling so high this morning, suspended in the ethereal hope that lifted us both. Now here I was, weighed down by the reality of our differences. The burden of clarity, regardless of the lingering tingle in my fingers.

I didn't want to think Anaisa was wrong with all her messages. I didn't want to disregard my instinct. But how could there be anything but this weekend between Emile and me? Today proved our differences.

It made no sense for me to hit him up, and I wasn't sure working with him made sense after all we had this weekend. The thought of Fridays without Emile made my stomach contract, lead settling in for the long haul.

I attempted to rally, singing at the top of my lungs with my girls, but my heart wasn't in it. The food dissolved on my tongue, the aftertaste of disappointment and unfulfilled dreams saturating my mouth.

"Girl, you look like you just found out plantains became an extinct species," Juju whispered.

"God forbid." I crossed myself, a shiver of dread kissing my spine.

"Why don't you go after him?" she asked, getting straight to the point.

The temptation of going back to Emile's skated down my back, the tingling in my fingers intensifying at the mere thought of him.

"I won't because he clearly needs space, and I'm not about to chase nobody." I shook my head, the words a struggle to say.

"Kiki…" Juju quirked her brow, then, with a gentle smile, nudged me, her touch warm on my shoulder. "Why are you so set on not letting that man in?"

If she only knew.

"Trust me, I let him in alright," I mumbled, but she missed it, having been pulled by Marsh and some of his annoying comments.

My attempts to shake my mood were unsuccessful.

The cold from outside kept sneaking into the restaurant and suddenly into my warm dress as well.

"Y'all, I'mma split. I got another spot to be at and..." Ephraim stood up.

"Boooooo. You always do this!" Juju complained as Ephraim went around the table, dapping hands and granting hugs. Any other time, I'd join Juju in her protest. As he waved goodbye, exiting the restaurant, an invisible hand pressed on my back, urging me forward until I rose from my seat.

"I'm gonna leave too. I haven't been home since Friday. I'll Venmo you, Juju."

"What? For real, you're gonna leave?" Lina's wide eyes, combined with Juju's frown, confirmed how out of character my behavior was. Great, Emile had me acting a fool in less than three days.

Three days? My palms flashed cold, then a pleasant warm as I allowed myself to accept the reality. I was down bad because I made a gamble on what it could be with Emile after fighting the urge to tumble into love for months. Regardless, it had happened, undetected, the way water claims its shores back from a man-made seaboard. Inevitable.

"Yeah, sorry for flaking. I'm just..." I shrugged, trailing off, not having the words to explain.

Juju studied me pensively, then nodded. Lina narrowed her eyes, and I braced myself for pushback, but it didn't come. She pursed her lips and pointed at me with her fork.

"You better spill what's wrong with you tomorrow, you hear me?"

"Yeah, yeah." I waved her a kiss, and she smiled, translating exactly what I meant. *Thanks, hun, for understanding, I love you, and I promise we will talk tomorrow when I'm in a better mental place.* Sometimes you didn't need much to explain.

The cold that continued to threaten me inside greeted me on the sidewalk, and I leaned into it. The dry leaves scent of this time of year invaded me, and I closed my eyes, taking stock, my head clear, my heart heavy.

"Abu, que susto!" I stumbled back after crossing the threshold of my house, the vibrant orange glint of Abu's cigar gleaming in the otherwise dark apartment. I clutched my chest, attempting to slow my heart's race to home plate. I stared at the apartment number next to my door, then back inside, taking one last glance for good measure.

Right, so I *am* in my apartment.

"Tu que hace aqui?"

"What, your Abu can't visit anymore?" She answered my question with a question, and I rolled my eyes.

"Abu."

"I saw that eye roll... I've been waiting for you. Where you been?"

I swear...

"Abu, I'm not a kid no more. This is why I moved out of your apartment with Mai."

"And why you moved to the building right in front, to really show us."

Air. That's what I needed. If I inhaled and exhaled enough times, I would chase away my not-yet calm heartbeat, as well as the annoyance coursing through me.

"Listen, I don't need your brand of rationality right now." I flicked on the light in my living room, my eyes adjusting to find Abu sitting by the window, the sill slightly open to let the smoke out. I should rat her out to Mai.

"I heard that," she warned, then took a deep inhale of her cigar, letting the rich aroma spread through the house.

"Get out of my head, Doña," I chastised her, knowing well she couldn't read my thoughts... Well, fifty percent sure she couldn't read my thoughts.

Walking to her, I plucked the cigar out of her fingers, inhaling deeply, the smoky sweet flavor of the tobacco leaves merging with my tastebuds.

"Did you give that boy the bites?" The cold from outside settled in my bones in one swoosh at Abu's question.

I always wondered why Abu didn't initiate as Mama Mambo.

"No, I didn't pack them with me."

"I packed them in your bag."

Pero que vidajena, meddling old...

"Watch yourself, you think I don't know you? That

face of yours…and you think too loud." It was Abu's turn to chastise me. I crumpled on my sofa, avoiding her intense eye contact.

"So, que paso?"

"He's wonderful, Abu. All I feared and dreamed." I traced the line of my eyebrow back and forth, feeling an odd comfort as I combed the hairs repeatedly.

"I told you."

"You basically told me to mount him." I finally stared at her, her smirk too much to bear right now.

"That I did."

"So, we were together the whole weekend. And it was comfort and familiarity and sex and warmth. All of it." All those feelings came rushing back at the memories of him. I continued as Abu's smirk softened into a pensive smile. "I didn't realize I was already falling for him, but I think you knew. Today, we woke up, and I remembered it was my brunch with my crew. We went out, and he…he was so overstimulated he walked out, leaving me behind."

"Mhm. See, I knew he should have tasted the bites."

Pero que carajo…what did the bites have to do with anything?

"Pero Abu…" Oh, shit. An icy trickle started at the top of my head, shimmering down my body. I opened and closed my mouth, impressed at the way she had of expecting these things. She'd explained once she didn't always understand why her instinct told her to do something, but the answer always presented itself. Always.

"I see you realize it."

My phone vibrated, and I saw it was Emile.

Emile: Hey, I thought you'd be here by now. Sorry I had to leave like that. What do you want for dinner?

Wow, he really thought leaving me behind like that was alright. I mean, the apology was nice, but that was it? The coldness returned, accompanied by an intense need to punch something.

Me: Nah, I came back to my crib. I'll stop by tomorrow to get my stuff.

I saw the three dots dance, then retreat three times.

Then…

Emile: Ok

I read and reread his text, the same sour feel in my mouth returning, the difficulty to form words taking over.

"What did you do?" Abu asked.

Just as I turned to her, my door swung open. I whipped my head to the opposite side, my heart not able to take so many gymnastics. Mai's loud voice and my Dad's lower tones followed as they entered my apartment.

I really miscalculated moving this close to my Mai and Abu. What did a girl need to do to get some peace?

"No, please. Let yourself in, why don't you?"

"Que? I used my key." Mai flashed me her key ring. I counted to ten in Spanish and then in English, just to avoid getting bopped for saying something rude.

"That was for emergencies!"

"This was an emergency! You didn't sleep here for two nights." Mai stomped, then stormed over to Abu, jerking the cigar out of her fingers and stubbing it out in the ashtray next to her.

Yikes, she's mad.

A pang of guilt ran through me, but then I remembered I was thirty-one years old, and I could, if I wanted, sleep somewhere that wasn't my house! They almost got me. Wao.

"Que tu quiere, Mai?" I asked, hoping whatever they needed was quick enough so I could go take a shower and crawl into bed.

"Hold up, what's got into you?" Mai peered at me, studying me as if I was one of her new recipes at the restaurant.

"Nada, Mai."

"Baby, what's wrong?" Dad asked, and the cold coalesced, shooting fast through me and converging behind my eyes. The prickle made me blink twice. My vision blurred as I thought of Emile and his last response.

"Your daughter fell in love with the boy she massages each Friday."

"Si, and?" Mai asked as if that was old news.

Rude.

"And well, he left me at boozy brunch without a backward glance."

"There's more to it than that," Abu warned. Ugh, why did people need to use rational thinking in these moments?

"Fine, he got really overstimulated by the noise and couldn't take it. But that proves what I feared all along.

I'm loud, and a lot, and noise follows me. All my life, people have shushed me, told me I speak too loudly, I do too much. Imagine if one Sunday at brunch overwhelmed him. He's allowed, but then what does that mean for anything for us?" My heart pounded in my chest as I spilled my fears to my family. Mai plopped herself next to me, and Dad crouched in front of me, their love holding up my walls.

"Ah, mi vida. You're not too much," Dad said.

"You always told me when I was home that I was too loud." I stared at him and saw him rear back—then I saw the moment he realized what I said was true.

"Sorry, baby. I just... Yeah, you're right, but I didn't mean it the way I made you feel. And that's a horrible excuse, but I'm sorry. I'm sorry that I put my needs in front of yours."

"What do you mean?" I asked, puzzled.

"You know I don't do as well as you and your Mai in loud family gatherings and parties. It's because I'm like that boy. Sensitive. Noise bothered me more than what is the average."

"I know you're an introvert, but you go out with Mai. Not even two weekends ago, you were at Tio Luchi's party."

"Si, but that's because Tio Luchi had a quiet area in his guest house in that backyard. The party was inside, but whenever your dad needed a break, he could go to the little shack in the back. That's what we've done for years. Strategize where he can have some quiet time," Mai said, sharing a knowing look with Dad. How were they still divorced?

"Si, your mom always found nooks and crannies, and if there wasn't, I stayed outside."

Realization dawned on me. How could I have been so oblivious to this? I always thought Dad was in the middle of the parties, but now that he said it, I remembered many times, searching for him and not finding him, to turn around twenty minutes later to find him by the bar chatting.

"Your Dad and I are polar opposites in a lot of things, but in the years, we found compromise." She gathered me to her, holding me from the side.

"Si como San Miguel a lado de Santa Ana," Abu said from her perch. I immediately understood her message. She used the syncretized names of Our Metresa Anaisa, who worked very well with Lwa Belie Belcan, despite their differences.

The tingle in my fingers increased, the feelings so intense my breath caught. My gaze found Abu, who beamed, then stared at the door.

CHAPTER

FIFTEEN

EMILE

The dark night loomed in front of me as I sat by my window in the main room. The view of New York never grew old, but today, it lacked its normal magic.

I'd fucked up.

I'd assumed that the days we'd spent together and Keyiara's understanding of me meant she knew what places like that restaurant could do to me. I'd misunderstood her concern.

In the restaurant, she'd checked on me, holding my hand, keeping me grounded, so I'd thought she knew. All she did, it helped for a bit, but sometimes nothing works. Today was one of those days.

I was far from perfect, and I had handled today horribly. And I'd wanted to talk to her in person, apologize, promise it would never happen again, but I never got the chance.

I sat with a beer in hand, the lingering feeling of defeat sitting heavy in me. I didn't want to give up on us when things were finally taking shape.

Quitting wasn't in my nature. Testing software for a living required a certain amount of patience and stubbornness to push through the hard days. But somehow, Keyiara left me in uncharted territory with no coding that I knew to work. This was all brand new to me. The sensation of fullness in my chest, the warmth in my stomach, the electricity in my veins. And let's not talk about the erections.

How could I get us back to our systems speaking to each other seamlessly?

I stood up, knowing that sitting here nursing my beer, feeling sorry for myself wasn't the answer.

It was early evening, and showing up unannounced at her apartment was probably a creep move. I had her address from the contract I had her sign at the beginning before I knew she was as trustworthy as the people I loved the most. Now she was part of that group. I didn't want to compound her annoyance with me with stalker behavior.

I paced the floor of my apartment back and forth, turning ideas in my mind of how to reach her, how to get her to see *me*. Maybe if Daymond hit her up for breakfast or lunch, I could then join them. It was still a bit creepy but less stalkerish. Well, slightly less... Scratch that. I could just go to her mom's restaurant and hope for the best.

Yes, I liked it. That idea had more merit. It meant I had to wait until the morning, though...

The warmth of my apartment caressed my bare feet as I paced. The pacing kept me grounded. It helped keep the determination at bay to go to her now. To talk to her now. To hold her now.

A sharp knock on the door froze me in my tracks. I pushed air out of my lungs as I approached, hoping whoever it was kept it brief.

I swung the door open, and my stomach somersaulted at the sight of Keyiara.

"Hey."

"Hey." I dragged a hand to the back of my head, the memories of the last few days rushing in with her return.

Then I remembered her massage table and bag were here, and the somersault became a cliff dive.

"I...can I come in?"

"Sure." I stepped aside, her verbena scent trailing around her as she walked by me with a little paper bag in her hand. She approached her massage table in the area by the loft's window, hovering around with her back to me. I refused to move far from the door, unwilling to hope she was here to stay longer than retrieving her things.

"I...I figured I'd stop by and bring you one of my Kiki Bites." She shook the paper bag in her hand, her face still, and that glimmer of hope ignited again.

"Thanks, I...I can't wait to try them." I nodded, my throat tight.

"Today was..."

"Today was how I want to start all my days." It was pointless to pretend or mince words. She was here, and I would say what I had to say, and at least I'd have the comfort I went down fighting.

"The start was bomb..." Her eyes clouded in recollection, then sharpened again. "Today was not how I thought I'd handle us going out together."

"Today isn't how I thought it would go, our first time out like that. But I'm not gonna lie, it could happen again. Are you ok with that?" I took a few steps toward her, helpless to the call of her aura.

"Yeah, yeah, I'm good. I realized there's ways we can navigate where we are different and still let this," she gestured between us, "thrive. I was just in my feelings, you know. I felt you left me behind, but I forgot for a moment what it felt like for you. And my parents might have given me a few tips for the next time."

"I'm so sorry I made you feel that way. In the moment, I thought we were on the same page, and I should've checked with you. I'll make sure to remember that. So, no more penetration testing, you're all in?" Two more steps, the rush of adrenaline spiking as I awaited her response.

"Ahh... I mean, if that's what you... I mean, I do like penetration, but we can talk it through." She wrung her hands, but she tried to mask her concern, and I busted out laughing. Damn, she'd really tried to rally, and I appreciated that gesture. It meant she really respected my spectrum of asexuality, and that glimmer exploded into fireworks.

"Nah, see, you interpreted what we were doing together as us testing my skills. But really, this was you testing if I was good enough for you. If my software and its oddities worked with your software and its own oddities. I've always known it would work, but you..." I wiped out the space between us, the rush of air in and out of her mouth detectable. Her face opened up, her body vibrating.

"I needed a little more reassurance. Let's just say today's test was a bit of a disaster." Her tinkling laugh was the kind of sound I always wanted to hear.

"It was, but you know what I've learned?" I leaned into her, her face tilting back, my eyes trained on her lush mouth.

"What?"

"That we can always try again tomorrow."

"Damn, Kiki, these bites are fucking amazing." I surged into her snug, wet— Oh, I really was going to nut in her fast. Kiki under me was the eureka moment when all the coding flowed perfectly and the test came back with zero problems. Kiki under me was a homecoming, the most familiar thing in the world. She was the fabric of dreams and the foundation of hope. With slow strokes, we undulated on my bed, her sienna skin glowing under the moonlight glinting through the window.

"Stay with me, Emile." She laughed as she threw her head against the pillow, the tendons of her neck inviting me to press kisses right in that nook where her essence was the most concentrated.

"I'm with you...can't you feel this dick?"

"Oh my god, you're a trip high."

"And you are a gift. A fucking amazing gift." I might be high, but it was all on her, on the fact that she returned and gave us another opportunity.

She moaned in my ear as I pressed my entire body against her, the tension in my lower half signaling the impending orgasm.

"Kiki...I need you to come."

"If you keep calling me Kiki, I sure will."

"Kiki...this wouldn't have worked with anyone else. Making love to you...it was only meant to happen like this...with you." My voice cracked as her walls hugged me. She enraptured me with her gaze full of wonder and love. I bit her bottom lip, then swooped in for a kiss so encompassing it left us both breathless.

"Oh, Emile, I love you too. I love making love to you. I love spending time with you." She gasped as I answered her declaration with a languorous stroke until no space remained between our two souls.

"Kiki, I love you." She quivered under me, around me, within me, and I succumbed to her moans, her orgasm calling mine.

"So, what are we doing tomorrow?" I pushed my weight off her, plopping in bed next to her, and she laughed beside me.

"Let's try Monday brunch. I think that will be way more relaxed."

"You get me, woman, you get me." And I gathered her close, knowing the beginning was full of possibilities as long as Keyiara was next to me.

ACKNOWLEDGMENTS

Thanks to Katrina and Tasha for spearheading this anthology. A year later, the need is still there.

Access to clean water is a human right.

For more information about the organizations that received the donations, please visit:

<u>Mississippi Reproductive Freedom Fund</u>

<u>Cooperation Jackson</u>

ABOUT THE AUTHOR

A.H Cunningham is an introvert that weaves lovey-dovey contemporary romance and erotica. Her characters are Black and Multicultural adults, trying to navigate their grown folk lives while contending with all the horny feelings and falling hopelessly in love in their journey. In her writing, you will find a deep love for the entire Black Diaspora and all the ways we connect through our heritage. When she's not writing, you can find her reading, snacking at odd hours, dancing some Panamanian song.

Join A.H's newsletter to get all the latest updates! http://www.ahcunninghamauthor.com

ALSO BY A.H. CUNNINGHAM

The Firecracker Cousins Series

Alight

Ablaze

Embers

Toying with Temptation

Holiday Shorts

'Tis The Season to Release

Wicked Moves Series

Plié

A Turn in the Air

Hidden Desires Series

Jardel

Check out the A.H. Universe website to see how it all connects!